All the best things I have in *my* life, aren't actually things!

What I need the most in *my* life, is *time*.

Time to feel emotions,
Time to feel someones touch,
Time to hear someones laugh,
Time to be in the presence of that special someone.

I would give anything to be able to stop *time* for a while, to sit, breath, listen and appreciate how great life actually is.

One

I am sat in yet another coffee shop, slowly stirring my tea and watching others go about their business. The stiff collar on my shirt irritating me as it has done all morning, but with a particular itch that I just can't stop. In and out walk the various coffee shop customers and then there's me, just sitting here contemplating life and how friggin hard it is.

At no point when I was growing up did anyone say it would be like this, this hard emotionally, or in any other way. Yes, during my teenage years I realised we all had to get jobs and work, so we could pay the bills and have a car, a tv or holidays or all of them. At no point did I realise that working to pay for all those things and being able to have all those things, would mean nothing! What I now know is all the best things I have in life aren't actually things! The thing I miss and need the most are time, or emotions that are felt from just being with someone. Someone's touch, hearing their laugh or just simply being in their presence. Time to stop the world for a while and just sit, breath, listen and appreciate what life can and should be.

I realise though, that I am incredibly lucky to be sat right here, in yet another coffee shop. I have been incredibly lucky in life generally, although on paper it wouldn't appear that way. On paper it would look like a complete disaster of a life, a waste of time, energy and emotions, but to me I feel lucky to have made it this far. There have been times when I couldn't afford to feed myself, there have been times where I was completely alone, so even though life is incredibly hard, I always remind myself of how lucky I am. I'm not rich by any means, but if I want a bottle of wine, or a takeaway, then I can afford it, which, as I tell myself constantly, not everyone can do and this is how I know I'm lucky.

My earliest memory would be aged about five, I suppose. Playing cars and train tracks in nursery with lots of other children and of course back then, I didn't have a care in the World. Life was simple, sleep, eat, play, cuddle and repeat. My life was all in front of me and I felt no stress, I didn't even know the word! One day we had a new playmate and in walked a black girl called Bonnie, as I found out, once she was introduced to the group. What I remember vividly are two things :

Firstly, this was the first black person I had ever seen and for the first time, I was aware that people could have different skin colour.

Secondly, I was aware that because her skin was a different colour most of the other children didn't want to play with her. I remember this confusing me, making me feel angry and I didn't remember having these feelings before that moment.

Looking back at this, of course I now realise what was going on. It's bizarre that children aged four or five can act this way, after all we are not born racist, or even know any different, but yet here I was feeling uncomfortable in the situation. So I did the only thing I felt I could do, which was to just be myself and to ask her to play. Sure enough Bonnie was a wonderful girl, a wonderful playmate and she turned out to be my first girlfriend. I am forever thankful that I acted the way I did. Bonnie became the most popular girl in school and I was her friend and eventually, I would become her husband. I believe these experiences have put me on a good footing for life, as I now like (or even dislike I suppose) a person for who they are and how they behave to me and not because of their skin colour, or religion or sexuality. This in turn has led me all the way to where I am today, which is sat right here in a coffee shop, watching the world come and go.

My job is like any other job, once you have learned the basics you just get on with it. Yes you get better at it and you learn more over time, which in turn means you get better again. However it doesn't matter who I'm speaking to, as each business is unique and for me to be able to help them, I need to spend time with them. This way I can really get to know them and their business. I'm always very interested in the people at the business, because I like people. I like finding out about people's lives and I'm a great reader of body language or situations. In my life, I have lived in lots of different places and experienced different ways of living, which I believe means I can adapt to most people. What I really like is when I've worked someone out and have already found a connection and just drop it into the conversation - the hook. It could be a place they live in, kids, sport, tv show, whatever and the reaction, the connection, is always worth the hunt. Then the selling of the product almost takes care of itself. As I say over and over again in meetings..... people buy people! That part where I can have a genuine connection with a person is interesting, the rest, is just a job!

This morning I woke up like any other day at six thirty, I jumped, or in reality flopped, out of bed and headed to the kitchen to start making the kids lunch boxes and clear the dishes from the night before. Different day, same jobs over and over. Bonnie also gets out of bed, goes to wake the twins, then gets herself ready. We both rush around seamlessly until Bonnie leaves at seven thirty for her job in the government building, in the city. Monday to Friday is always the same, although in fairness Saturday and Sunday are also very similar, it's just me taking the kids to their various clubs and being Mr Taxi. The evenings are just as crazy, as I arrive home, it's a quick change and back out with the twins to swimming, football or whatever is on that night. Occasionally I get chance to eat before I head back out, but this hardly ever happens as a family, as we just don't get the time to match up and usually I eat late in the evening.

On weekdays I drop the twins off to school in the morning, then head to my office or to my meeting with clients. Usually the boss calls to see what sales figures I have for her and as usual they are never good enough. If I want to keep my job, I need to up my game. I have no idea what my game is, other than parenting and trying to find that connection to the person sat in front of me and of course to pay the bills. I often think about how I used to be a funny, happy guy. I would make people laugh (I think) I would enjoy the job and nothing bothered me. If the job became too hard or just plain boring, I would lie about my position, by saying I was doing the next position up from me, or my current company had promised me the next position up and then I was let down. Therefore I would leave the company to pursue my next role and I would nearly always get the job, for more money and would be happy again for a few years. Richard Branson once said, take the job even if you don't know how to do it, you can learn how to do it. In fairness that motto has never let me down.

Now though, I'm in my mid forties, still trying to keep fit by playing squash with my old school buddy, George. We let off steam every week, not by exercising, but by moaning about our jobs, house, age etc but it gets us through another week. Yes, being honest I have a little beer belly, but generally I'm not in that bad a condition. The biggest problem I have is that I don't know who I am anymore , the cheeky carefree bloke has gone and instead he has been replaced, by "Mr businessman", in a suit, with responsibilities and spreadsheets and targets. How the friggin hell did that happen! I even have voices in my head constantly telling me life is crap, you need to give up, you need to switch off the phone and go rogue. I'm like yeah, let's do it and then a client calls, I answer the phone and tell them everything is great, which to the outside World it probably looks that way. Nice house, family, holidays, cars on the driveway, what's not to like? However, that pressure to provide, is slowly eating me up. It's devouring me from the inside, but it's gobbling me up, one day at a time all the same. Little by little I'm disappearing and a new, boring middle aged person looks back at me in the mirror, looking greyer, older, more stressed and less sparkle in my eyes!

So this morning after the school run I've headed here, to my meeting in this little coffee shop, to meet a prospective client, so I can go through the same routine again. The "hi how's it going", or the "strange weather we're having" chats, before we move on to talk about the latest tv shows. Slowly, but surely, finding something to connect with.

I've arrived early and I'm sat here stirring my tea, contemplating life. Then in walks a smart, powerful but hippy looking lady, right on time and she heads straight to meet me. This part always amazes me.... I've only spoken to her briefly on the phone, she explains how she got my number, usually one of my clients has said I've done some great work for them and she should give me a call. We agree a time and a place to meet, exchange a few niceties in the hopes I can find something to connect with and then we hang up. Now here's the bit I don't get, I'm sat in a coffee shop, a coffee shop full of people, some are mums with children, some are retired folk, some are business people having meetings, like me. Some are men some are women sitting by themselves, sat waiting for someone, or they are just sat here taking a break from their day. The point is, I'm not sat there with a great big sign saying sales man this way, but always and I mean always the new prospective client will walk in, spot me and come right up to me saying "hi, you must be Greg, we spoke on the phone". How the hell does that happen?

So, in walks my connection to be, hippy looking but normal for this part of town. Everyone who lives around here likes to look cool, although I'm not even sure the word cool, is even cool anymore. I try to stir my tea and not look her way, it might not even be the person I'm meeting - after all we've never met, so this lady could be anyone. Then sure enough she keeps walking right towards me, smiling and says "hi, you must be Greg, we spoke on the phone". I would love to say straight back, "how the friggin hell did you know it was me, do I have, I'm a sales idiot tattooed on my head"? But instead I immediately stand up, offer my hand and say "hi" back, followed quickly with, "please take a seat". It's always weird meeting someone of the opposite sex, for the first time, are you supposed to kiss them on the cheek, are you supposed to kiss both cheeks? Or as I do, offer my hand? I usually keep it formal, as I don't want to get it wrong from that very first meeting. We do the usual gesture for more teas or coffees and then we can start with the pleasantries, before moving towards the business discussion. I can always throw in some more pleasantries when I need to change the subject, or allow myself time to think, then get back to the business part. As I often say, this should just feel like a chat, as I need to understand the person and their business, before I can even start to think about the solutions .... after all people buy people don't they!

However, Annie St Hillier was to be a very different person to meet. Annie starts to play the game, the niceties, the weather and moves onto business all before the tea has even arrived. "I appreciate you meeting me this morning", she says, which is usually my line. "Also meeting me first thing, as I'm sure you'd have preferred to go into the office, straight after the school run and meet later in the day, but this time works better for me today. Time, you see Greg, is a strange thing. We all think we have lots of it when we are young, we feel we will live forever and then all of a sudden we are in our mid forties and we start worrying that we are running out of time". I have to admit it, my head has turned already and instead of trying to find a connection, Annie has just smacked me right in the face with her version of one. I feel like a 15 year old boy staring at a picture of Kelly Le Brock, I can almost feel my jaw dropping open and what's worse, Annie knows it.

Annie has this strange look about her, a kind of subtle, but very sure look of I've got you right where I need you. "My business", she continues, "is time". Leaning forward in the chair, Annie continues, "most people think they want flash cars, or expensive houses, but the truly rich just want more time, more time with their family, more time to do those jobs around the house that they can't do, because they are working all the time. Time for holidays, time for experiences, time for themselves to go and play sport with a friend, time to be alone with their wife, time my friend, is the most valuable thing in the world right now. Time is what we all need more of and time, if used wisely, can change everything".

Am I dreaming, or is Annie really sat in front of me steam rolling the meeting? Am I really sat here like a fifteen year old boy, with absolutely no words coming out of my mouth, no matter how much I try. Eventually I take a sip of my tea, trying to look calm and intrigued, without my gawking fifteen year old's face. Another thing I tend to do a lot when I'm losing a discussion, or when I simply want to get the meeting back to my way of thinking, is to reply with, "I completely agree with you". So this feels like the right thing to do here, quickly followed by, "if only it was that simple? Life seems to take over though doesn't it? One moment we are young and carefree, then it seems in the next moment, we have a mortgage, kids and way too much debt to stop working. The need for time, becomes the need for more time, so I can earn more money, after all, we have way too much to lose now".

Annie smiles and puts down her drink agreeing with me. "You are absolutely right", she says, "but my business is all about time and I want you to come onboard to ensure we are using our time wisely. Look, you can stay in your job until you retire, you can keep trying to hit the targets, even though they increase them every year. You can pay the bills, keep the kids in their school clubs and their video games, hell you can even play squash occasionally, but you know deep down, you, need, more, time! You need the old you back, the happy person you've lost along the way, the stress free you. Now let's just imagine I can offer you all that and you get more free time than you can ever remember. You only come to work when you've had enough holidaying, when you are looking for the next challenge, when you are really ready to work. More money than you can dream about, but most importantly, with this offer comes the time you crave! What do you say? Why not come and work for us, at Tx3"?

It's strange to be presented with a meeting like this. Your first thought would always be to grab the offer with both hands and run around shouting hallelujah from the top of your voice. However the reality is, you don't think it's real, or that it's even

course. I email Annie to confirm the time and date, but don't send it until Thursday morning, as I don't want to appear too eager. Annie confirmed the meeting and also advised a car will be sent to pick me up on Monday morning at ten.

The weekend comes and goes with sports clubs and parties for the twins and before I know it, Monday morning has come around. I am up and about doing the usual routine, when I realise I am a little nervous about the meeting. I never get nervous about interviews, or meetings in general, so this is a new feeling for me. I guess this is a sign that I want this job quite badly, maybe because it appears to be an opportunity of a lifetime. I soon have the twins in school and I am back at the house spending a few minutes getting myself ship shape and ready. The doorbell suddenly rings at nine fifty eight and I know this is it. I take a few deep breaths, look in the mirror and tell myself, "you can do this", like it will help. I open my front door, to be greeted by my driver waiting for me. A red headed woman in a black suit and she is even wearing a chauffeurs hat, the type you see the driver wearing for rich people. I am about to be one of those so called, rich people, for the first time in my life. The car itself is a really slick looking Mercedes, shiny silver with tinted windows at the rear. The type of car that I can't afford to service, let alone own. I really want to sit in the front passenger seat, with the driver next to me, so we can chat, as I would normally do, when using a taxi. This of course, is not a taxi and as I approach the car I am directed into the back, where it can only be described as, complete luxury.

The journey takes a little over an hour and I am familiar with most of the roads, as it isn't exactly too far from home. Then the car turns off the main road, onto a quieter side road and eventually onto a private road. The entrance is set with a grand wall and what appears to be electric gates which are already open. Maybe the electric gates, are just fixed gates and here for the affect. The forest lined private road meanders along for about half a mile and eventually opens up to a magnificent, modern style semi-circle shaped building, with a long sweeping driveway in front of it. In front of the driveway is a pond with waterfalls spraying their arcs, along with brightly coloured plants, that take my breath away. As we slow, a man approaches, from the main entrance to greet me, smiling, but acting like I am the boss or certainly a VIP, which let's be honest, couldn't be further from the truth. "Good morning Sir, welcome to Tx3", he announces, as he ushers me into the building. "Can I get you a drink while you wait"? Normally I would accept a drink, after all I hang out in coffee shops a lot for my job, but I am still feeling a little nervous and I'm not sure when I will get to the toilet next, which is age thing, as I politely decline.

As we enter through a great glass door with very tall glass walls, I am presented with some old race cars, parked inside, for goodness sake. To me they look like old formula one cars, but I suppose they could have been any old race cars. I am drawn to a particularly fetching red and white, single seater car and I read the plaque that stands in front of it. It simply reads, Ayrton Senna, McLaren. Now that is a name I instantly recognise and I realise this is the second car I have seen up close today, that I can't afford. The place, as I glance around is truly amazing and I wonder what sort of money this company make from selling "time", as it has been put to me.

Annie St Hillier walks towards me smiling and holding out her hand, which I gratefully except. As we shake hands, Annie pulls me into her, gesturing me to kiss her cheek, which is unexpected. It would be awkward if I leave her hanging, so I dutifully kiss her cheek and we say "hi", almost at the same time. Annie is dressed immaculately and smells just as immaculate, which makes me feel slightly intimidated, in terms of my own dress sense and aftershave, which I'd been given as a birthday present from the twins earlier this year. Annie is however, very nice and makes a big effort to welcome me into the business. Quickly pointing out that, "I want you to relax, feel comfortable and ask as many questions as you want". I'm just starting to feel a little relaxed, as Annie continues, "today", she says, "is not a job interview, as I'm sure you would have thought of it that way. In simple terms we want you, so the role is yours if you want it. My job today is to show you enough of what we do, how we do it and of course where you fit into all this. We have spent the last few months researching you, your family and your lifestyle to know we have the right person for this role, I only ask that you keep an open mind please".

I'm suddenly very thrown by this, as yet again I'm not used to this happening. I'm not in control of the meeting, which doesn't sit well with me and again Annie knows this, I'm sure. We walk though to the rear of the building, I can see right through, as there is a glass wall at the rear of this incredible building, as well as the front. Out of the glass, in the distance, I see a lawned area, some tennis courts to the side and an area which I imagine would be used for events or gatherings. In simple terms, this is easily the most magnificent building I have ever set foot in and it's a far distant cry from my current office, which has old fashioned desks and chairs. The most modern thing in our office is Skype, which has recently been installed and yet no one knows how to use it.

We arrive at the rear of the building, which is clearly Annie's office. It has a wonderful view of the lawned area and a very long boardroom style desk, a sofa and what appears to be a private bathroom. Annie leads me to the sofa and not the big boardroom style desk, as would normally happen in these situations. Considering this is an office sofa and I assume, hardly sat on, it is much more comfortable than the one we have at home. I shouldn't be surprised I suppose, but I am. Annie smiles, "do you think you could get to like it here? In fairness you wouldn't be here very often, but when you do need to visit, I want you to feel proud of where you work".

"During our walk around I will show you a few spaces where I think your office can be and you can let me know which one you'd prefer. For now though, let me tell you a little about this company, what we are trying to achieve and the role we know you are perfect for. Once we have finished, I can give you a demonstration to really bring it all to life. Finally, I have been a little presumptuous, sorry and I have asked for your company car to be brought here today. Assuming you are happy to join us, then you might as well drive yourself home later. After all of this and to pre-warn you, I will be asking you how you feel, if you're in, or out? I will be looking for some sort of commitment and yes, I appreciate you may want to discuss this at home, but I would appreciate your feedback at that point". My response is as considered and as polite as possible, but deep down inside I am screaming yes I will take it, I will take the job right now.

Then however, a great big thought slaps me in the face. What if this company is an illegal operation? Is this how they have so much money? What am I possibly getting myself involved with?

Three

Annie is like a child at Christmas, all excited to show me the business, the toys and gadgets they have for use. As much as the tour is exciting, it dawns on me that everything I am seeing is at a very high level. Lots of pretty shiny things, lovely people but no real substance. Nothing which actually explains, who they are, what they do and from a selfish perspective, nothing at all about what I would be doing. Yes, I hear lots about "Time", about technology and about how I can help save people lives, which sounds exciting, but nothing really tangible.

With the guided tour out of the way, we are on our way to lunch when a young, very smartly dressed man, approaches Annie with a welcoming smile. He hands a little box to me and says to Annie, "sorry to interrupt but she has just arrived and I must say" he continues, "that she looks incredible". I am clearly confused but Annie appears excited. "Come", Annie says, "let's take a look and see what you think. I'm like a little lamb following her to the front of the building, where I spot her for the first time and I have to agree with the young man, she does look incredible. I have never thought of a car as a he or a she before, they have always been things to get me to meetings or to drive the family around. If I'm being perfectly honest I've never been able to afford a nice car. I've always bought the best one I can and fit a private plate to it, so I can hide how old it really is. These days my car is never clean, always full of sweets and crisp wrappers and has football boots lying around. The car always smells of a musty, damp smell, that means I drive with the windows slightly open, in the hope I don't capture the smell on my suits. However, this car in front of me is a thing of beauty, an Aston Martin, of pure shining wonderfulness and excitement. It looks perfect and it looks like it's smiling from wheel to wheel.

Annie's face is a picture, her eyes are as round as the shiny wheels and her skin appears to be glowing, just like the paintwork. I feel slightly envious, but overall I'm pleased for her. After all Annie has clearly worked incredibly hard to build this company and she deserves this most wonderful reward, parked in front of us. I'm also aware that this is all a game, to show me that if I work hard for the company, then maybe one day, a car like this could be mine. It's the oldest trick in the management book, probably under item one of how to get your employees to work hard, so the owners get a big, healthy bonus! Annie asks if I'd like to sit inside, to which any of the professionalism I have left, disappears and I immediately confirm "yes". I think I say yes, even before Annie has finished the sentence. However as I walk around the car, Annie's face suddenly turns to confusion. Annie wants to know, "why are you going to the passenger side? how on earth are you going to drive it, if you sit that side"? with a slightly scrunched face. I laugh, a strange and nervous laugh, a laugh I've never heard come out from my body before, a genuine holy shit sort of laugh. "Why would you want me to drive your car? surely you will want to take her for a spin before anyone else does"? Annie's confused looking face relaxes, returning to normal, as she suddenly realises why I am heading for the passenger seat. "Greg, I don't think you realise what is happening here? this is your car, the car I was telling you about earlier, the one I thought you might like to drive home tonight". My face must look a picture, as I glance at the car, then at Annie and then back at the car again. I am embarrassingly lost for words. This is starting to turn into a habit and Annie yet again, has the upper hand. My earlier thought about this being a management trick is obviously wrong, but I don't feel embarrassed, I don't know what I feel, if I'm being honest. Probably the best way to describe how I feel, is an out of body experience, like this is all a dream. The young man nudges my hand, as I am still holding the box, "the key Sir, you have the key in the box". My brain finally catches up and processes the situation. Annie encourages me, "take the car for spin to see what you think". I slide in behind the steering wheel, hit the start button to hear a magical roaring noise, the type of which I have never heard before. I also feel a glorious vibrating rumble in my bottom, that I have never felt before. I drive away slowly at first and head back down the private road with the windows open so I can gulp in the powerful engine noise and enjoy every single second of this. I gradually put my foot down, increasing the speed quickly and this thing of beauty simply roars into life. It is easily the most powerful car I've ever been in and I will never have this feeling again, the feeling of driving this ultimate beauty of a car for the very first time. It is beyond any of those wildest dreams, that my fifteen your old self had, while sat in my bedroom. For the first time in years, I'm having the time of my life and I'm smiling again and I feel like I don't have a care in the World. I decide to stop the car as I reach the main road and gates and unexpectedly burst into tears. All the stress that has been building up for years, all the worries about keeping my job, so I can keep paying the bills and the stress I've had in keeping my family safe, is finally coming out. The raw emotion of feeling, as I have finally achieved something in my life and the relief in knowing that I am going to take this job, whatever this job is, so I can keep enjoying moments like this, is beginning to pour out of me. It's like I have been a broken man all along, who is finally able to start healing and for the first time in years I truly feel alive. Not only alive, but I am thankful to be alive and not just existing, while I go through the motions of the day!

I'm not sure how long I've sat here for, or how many tears I've cried, but every tear drop is worth it. I drive back to Annie, very calm, very happy with the time I've spent in finding myself again and very happy with the choice I am about to make. For the first time in years I feel incredibly happy with a thing, a car as it turns out and I am excited about the future. What this will mean for my family and how excited Bonnie will be when I get to tell her about my day, my new job, my new car and I suppose my new found me!

Four

As I return to the majestic building, Annie has returned to her office, as I am greeted just like the first time. I'm welcomed inside, "would you like a drink while you wait, Sir"? I not even sure the man realises I've been here most of the day. I accept a glass of water this time and wait next to the red and white car. Annie appears shortly afterwards with a wonderful smile, "did you enjoy your time in the car"? I nod enthusiastically and confirm, "it was incredible and it has certainly helped me to re-evaluate my current life". Annie is clearly pleased and wants to get down to the business end of the day. I am happy and relieved to finally find out about the job and what I will be required to do. Annie leads the way, by simply stating, in her words, "a few bullet points to whet your appetite and to demonstrate how serious we are in hiring you. Firstly", she states in a very matter of a fact way, "the wage, I know money is important to you but I also know that it's not all about money. Yes I know you want to support your family and make them as secure as possible but you also want time to spend with them. Gone are the days where you get to go home and put up your feet in the evening. There is always one club or another that you need to get to, right? And you sometimes skip off work early to ensure you get there on time. I also know that once the twins are in bed, you often open up your laptop and start work again, just so you can fit it all in".

As ever Annie is scarily accurate. "So, let's get the wages part out of the way : we will pay you four million pounds a year for this role". Am I going mad, did Annie just say I will get paid four million pounds and I didn't even flinch. Not because I am playing it cool, but because I am frozen, in shock, to my seat. As my brain tunes back in again, Annie continues, "I'm hoping this will take the pressure off you and your wife and life can become more.... well, manageable again".

I am still picking my jaw up from the floor, when Annie continues. "Secondly, as I've said before, you will be able to take as much time off work as you need and when you're ready you can report in for duty. What I want, is for you to want to work, to want to be here and want to help in changing the lives of millions of people. You can only do this if you are fully committed and ready, therefore you must holiday as much as you need to, so you can achieve this. This could be weeks or even months at a time". It's a good job Annie can't read my mind, or she would hear my brain screaming this woman is mad. I'm not worth four million pounds a year and if I can holiday as much as I want, then I will never be in work! "The perks", Annie continues, "like healthcare etc we can get into another day, but can we agree that this is a great way to start"?

I am yet again lost for words and just smiling like a Cheshire Cat and nodding like a stupid dog at the same time, which is another first for me. All of this is starting to freak me out, it's like some kind of joke. I simply thank Annie, "the terms seems generous" followed with, "I am slightly concerned about what I am expected to do, in order to receive this package". Annie seems pleased with my direct response, "Greg, whilst I would like to tell you everything about your role, I simply cannot, that is until you accept the position. What I can say is that all of us here at Tx3 are very happy with our choice in you. We know you are exactly the right person for the job and the way you have handled today, has only confirmed this. I think it will help to give you a little demonstration now, as promised, which will hopefully show you what we are all about. The role we want you to do is simple, we just want you to talk to the people we ask you to, about time and Tx3. In reality the job is pretty similar to what you do now, you meet people, get to know them and talk to them about the product, the offering if you like. The people you meet however, will not be easy to convince, but lives depend on you getting them to understand the benefits of joining up with us here at Tx3. Sounds straightforward right? But every time we send you off to meet someone, we are very keen for you to get the deal done. We cannot accept no for an answer, so it could mean you having to make several trips and that is why we are prepared to pay you handsomely. While you stay with your family we are happy for you to be with them, but when you are with us, we need you to be one hundred percent focused on getting the job done. This could take years in some cases but you must stick with the job until it is complete. Now I appreciate that sounds like a huge payoff... this could involve you being away from your young family for a few weeks or even months at a time, however each time you return we make sure, that in reality you have only been away for a few seconds. So from the outside it would look like you've come here to your office, in your new company car and then go home again, on the same day. To reassure you this is even possible and that we have all the time we want on our hands, please let me demonstrate. Greg, please welcome a very important person in this company, he is our President, in fact he is THE President. Greg please say hello to President John F Kennedy"!

Five

I guess the correct response when coming face to face with a President of the United States and a dead one at that, should be, "good morning Sir", or "good morning Mr President". I however look at him in complete disbelief. I laugh out loud and say "it's you, you're the dead president". Let's be honest this is not my finest moment in life! I glance at Annie as my confusion levels rise yet again, as my brain attempts to compute the fact that JFK is stood in front of me, alive and not looking any older than all the TV clips I'd seen of him, when being shot, back in November 1963.

JFK however, calmly walks forward, a cool smile on his handsome and cheeky looking face and offers out his hand, which I take in all its glory and wonderment. "Hi Greg", he says smoothly, "it's a pleasure to meet you. This must be a strange day for you? Let me just say, I'm am forever indebted to Tx3 and I will never regret making time to speak with them, it turned out to be invaluable! I will leave you finalise your contract with Annie and we can catch up the next time our paths cross. Welcome to your amazing new life in Tx3 and the amazing people you will meet, plus the wonderful places this job will no doubt take you to". With that he turns, smiling briefly at Annie and walks out of the room. My brain is trying to work out if it had really happened, or if I am going completely mad. "So"..... Annie says, "I think that concludes my demonstration. What do you think"?

Not for the first time since we met, I am completely lost for words. I try to gather my thoughts quickly and eventually I am able to reply with, "well that was certainly impressive", but that is about all I can get out of my dry mouth. Over the next hour, Annie gives me the rest of the guided tour and a very basic overview of my role. The role is defined as : attend various meetings with people, or targets as they are called, to get as close to them as possible. Once a relationship is struck and a true connection made, then I introduce Tx3 to them and of course the concept of time. Annie fills in the detail, "you will only work with one target at a time, so you can give them your one hundred percent attention. You need to get them to appreciate the product, why it is invaluable to them and why they need to buy-in to the concept. You will be fully debriefed about each and every target, but each one is specifically chosen because they can make a bigger impact on the World. If it takes you several years to convince them, then so be it. Each trip and indeed each target will be different. Sometimes you can be away for a day or a week and on the rare occasion, months at a time. However, you can return to Tx3 at any point, in the knowledge that you have in reality only been away for a few seconds. In terms of holidays you can take as much time off as needed, months even, but as far as your family are concerned you will need to pop into work for the odd day occasionally. Clearly your job is to highlight the benefits of time and Tx3, but only when you truly believe you can fully trust the target and they are ready". Annie casually drops in, "of course the worst that could happen, is the target tells everyone they have met a time travelling man, but we don't really want to deal with any fall out unless we really have to". My mind is still spinning, did Annie just say I would be time travelling? "Then once you have the buy-in from the target, a team will take over and repat them".

It is perfect, it is certainly exciting and terrifying, in equal measures. I still have plenty of unanswered questions, but realise I won't get the answers to those until I am fully onboard. I therefore conclude my day by signing the employee contract and shaking hands with Annie. The documents make it perfectly clear what I can say, or more importantly what I can't say to Bonnie, or anyone for that matter. I am however, extremely relieved to have it all completed and the decision made, so I can go home and tell Bonnie, as much as I can about my new job. After all, this will affect her life as much as mine. Life suddenly feels rosier and I can feel the pressure lifting from my shoulders as every second passes. Annie also seems delighted that I have taken on the job.

Annie's final parting shot is to confirm my employment, by depositing a cool five hundred thousand pounds into my bank account, as a "golden handshake" and she welcomes me into the company. As Annie puts it, "this will immediately release the financial pressures at home, you can also hand in your notice immediately and tell them you are not going to work there anymore". This money means I don't need to work any of my notice period either and I will be officially working for Tx3, as of tomorrow.

Six

As I head home, I think about how I will walk through the front door and announce my news to Bonnie. I want to share the excitement of my day and if I'm being honest I want to show her the car. I finally feel like I've landed, like I can prove to myself that I've made it. I don't mean financially, although if I'm being honest with myself, the money and the car certainly help. I want Bonnie to feel excited with me, like we have our lives back and life means something. I want to score brownie points and beat my chest, saying I've provided for my family, like some old caveman. I want Bonnie to be as excited as me and to also feel the pressure lift from her shoulders. I don't give a damn if she carries on working, it's not a chauvinistic thing, I just want to show her that life is good and stress free again and we can afford the nice things in life. The twins can have an amazing upbringing without the worries I've been having. I want Bonnie to jump up and down and if I'm being truly honest, I want Bonnie to want me sexually. Things have certainly been slow in that department for a long time.

Don't get me wrong, Bonnie is a fantastic mum, she gives one hundred percent attention to the twins. Unfortunately this means I no longer feature on her chart. Once the twins have gone to bed I want it to be "our time", without the twins interrupting every thirty seconds. The reality is we rarely have any uninterrupted time together and Bonnie doesn't seem that interested in me, even when we are alone, because she is tired from the day. I can't remember the last time Bonnie tried to hold my hand, or give me a cuddle. I've no idea when she last pinched my bottom or put her arms around me while I am chopping something in the kitchen. God forbid she try and kiss me, or make a pass at me. We have turned into the people in the house that just help with the twins and pay the bills. Every night though, I go to bed hoping, praying even, for sex. I still love my wife but even if I try it on, make my move or whatever it's called these days, I just get rejected, time after time after time. I no longer know what to say, without it sounding like I'm begging and it's eating me up inside.

However as I drive nearer to the house, I realise I'm actually feeling excited. I'm imagining how this will all play out. A few glasses of wine, maybe we can talk about holidays and how our lives might change, followed by a night of passion. Naked, skin to skin, hot sweaty passion. The type where

Bonnie climbs on top of me and takes control, maybe Bonnie will even put on some of her black sexy underwear, like she used to do. As I pull up onto our driveway, I'm grinning from ear to ear and my heart is beating very fast with expectation.

I walk through the front door and I'm just about to shout to Bonnie, but see the twins running around like they are high on sugar. Bonnie is in the kitchen trying to cook something up quickly and she is trying to get the twins to sit down at the table. This is supposed to be my moment, my big stop everything you are doing moment. Bonnie however quickly walks past me, half a smile as she reminds me we need to be at the first kids club in under an hour and the twins haven't changed or eaten their evening meal yet. Basically it is all going off and I have walked right into the perfect storm! My puffed out chest and car keys are quickly pushed to one side and my manhood deflated like a balloon at the end of a party. I decide in an instant to shut up, roll up my sleeves and just get on with being a parent. Bonnie doesn't even look up when asking, "how was your day"? and she will certainly not be listening to any answer I might give. So I don't give one. Bonnie has clearly forgotten I was going for a job interview today and is rightly giving all her attention to getting everything ready, as quickly as possible. I don't even hit the outer ring of the dart board, let alone the bullseye. I know I need to ignore my news and concentrate on getting the twins ready to leave for their club shortly. After all, the twins must always come first and a new job for daddy, or a lovely sounding car, doesn't really feature high up on the list at this particular moment.

The night goes by just like the others, me playing Mr Taxi, but in a much, much nicer car. It's strange how the dads spot your car and suddenly you are and have allegedly, always been, part of the group. Tonight I am elevated to a much higher position in the group and they are suddenly very interested in what I do. I decide to tell them I'm a managing director of a tech company, that supplies the government. They lap it all up and I like the fact that I can be whoever I want to be. After all, I can be on holiday for as long as I want and I have half a million in the bank! Life is just beginning to be great.

Once the twins have gone to sleep, I am finally sat in bed with Bonnie and start to tell her about my day. Bonnie quietly says "oh I'm sorry, I forgot to ask how your interview went", while rolling over, quickly followed with, "I'm really tired Greg" and finally, the mumbles of, "it sounds like it could be good for you". Im aware that I haven't spoken a single word in response to Bonnie and very quickly she is asleep.

In fairness, I'm usually the one falling asleep first, so it's strange to see this beautiful woman lying next to me sleeping, while I contemplate my day and my future. In reality, I didn't tell Bonnie anything, let alone about the car or the money side of things. The final nail in the coffin is no cuddling or intimacy, regardless of how I imagined it playing out. I am however alone, in the dark with my own thoughts, certain I did the right thing in accepting the job today. The excitement about the bizarre things I saw and want to celebrate, but I need to keep it all contained. What I do know is that I have hit the jackpot and I am praying Richard Branson is right this time. What I'm really not sure about, is if I can blag it again, at this level, with this amount of money on offer and being this close to becoming free, financially and emotionally. What I do know, is that I am going to give it absolutely everything I have within me and if all else fails I will drag the job out as long as I can. After all they are going to pay me so much money, that I won't need to be there for that long, before I can completely clear the mortgage and have enough savings to live out my days.

The morning soon arrives, to exactly the same routine as any other, except I drop the twins off at school and head straight back home. Bonnie left for work early and I assume she believes my day is going to be just like any other. My plan however, is much more simple, I have three tasks to complete throughout the day.

Task one, check my internet banking to see if five hundred thousand pounds has been received as promised. I need to be sure it isn't all some bizarre dream, or worse, some horrible trick being played on me. If the money is in my account, it will be proof that this is definitely happening. This will then lead me nicely onto my second task, which I am strangely not looking forward to.

Task two will then be to write my resignation and email it to my boss, so I will be free of my current job.

Then finally, task three is to call my boss and talk to her about my resignation and get any of her moans and groans out of the way.

I take a deep breath as I log in to my bank account. I can hardly look at the screen. I'm even tempted to look through my fingers like you do when watching a horror film, but then, there it is. The screen is glaring brightly at me, with the balance of my account jumping out at me and yes the big money has indeed been paid in. I immediately let out a strange noise of pure relief. I have not been made to look like a fool, I didn't dream it all and it is now officially day one of my new, cool life.

The day couldn't have started any better and I immediately start to type my resignation email as fast as I can. It's like it has to be emailed by a certain time, or my life depends on it. I am so happy and excited and the nerves have completely disappeared. I click send, before I can analyse what is happening and watch the email go into my sent items. That's it, its done, the start of my new life whisking its way around the internet. I decide to add a forth task to my to do list, which is to drive my new, beautiful car, to the coast and to enjoy the day. I can put on my shades and drive there without a stress in the World. I need to be back in time to pick up the twins from school of course, but that's hours away yet. The phone suddenly rings, causing me to jump out of my skin, it's my boss, "I've received your email" she shouts in my ear. The subject line is "Resignation", which kind of gives it away I suppose. I try to keep the conversation short and professional, starting with a simple, "good morning, you've received my email then"? My boss however is not in the mood for pleasantries and immediately starts moaning with the classic, "I hope this is some sort of joke"? I explain, "I've been given an opportunity that I simply cannot turn down, the decision has been made, no turning back now". The call is over very quickly and I agree to post all my work things back to the company, by the end of the week and that's it, finished. I am clearly just a cog in the company wheel and one that can easily be replaced.

I'm not good in these situations, but I'm determined for it not to bother me and that now means, New job, New life and hopefully a New me, well... the good old me back, anyway. I want to shout hooray, throw my fist into the air or something momentous, but I actually feel quite low. I'm not good at disappointing people and as positive as I was earlier, I actually feel melancholy, which completely throws me. I decide to scrap my forth task and just mooch about the house until it's time to pick up the twins from school.

Seven

I have accepted the best job in the World and have all the freedom I can ever want. I could take the next month off if I want to and I have money in the bank, to back all of this up. So why the hell do I have this yearning to go straight back to Tx3, to start work straight away? I suppose I want to know everything about the job and the project they have lined up for me, but it feels weird that I want to start immediately. If someone offered this deal to me in a pub, as a "play along scenario" like the ones where someone says, what would you do if you won fifty million on the lottery? Then I would have said, I will take the rest of my life off, after all the deal is I can have as much time off as I need and only go to work when I am ready to give it one hundred percent. But now I'm in this situation, I don't actually want that, I actually want to get to work straight away, which I bet is Annie's plan. Annie has always been one step, maybe more, ahead of me! I have already decided I will be driving back to Tx3 in the morning and I want to be ready. I don't know what I need to be ready for, so I can't train, or plan, not that I even have enough time, but I am determined to be ready.

The following morning, after the school run, I find myself climbing back into my wonderful car and heading straight back to Tx3. The day is a glorious, sunny type of day. I drive like I have all the time in the World. Usually after the school run, I rush back to the car and drive, all stressed, to my first meeting, or to the office. Every red light gets my blood pressure soaring higher and higher and the whole trip is usually just one big stress session.

Today though, I don't need to be at Tx3 for any particular time, I haven't even told Annie I am coming. For once I look like those wealthy, relaxed, people in expensive cars that pull up next to you at the lights. The same lights where I am usually sat all stressed out and these people annoyingly look like they've just come from the gym, followed by a trip to the hairdressers. I would sometimes glance at them and wonder if I could magically swap places with them and their lives for a few days, to see how happy they really are. I would convince myself that they are up to their eyeballs in debt and all this is just for appearances. Well today, it's my turn to look relaxed, in my new, shining, expensive car and today it's my turn to see others looking very stressed out. I thoroughly enjoy the weather, the music on the radio and of course the glorious sound of the engine. This is certainly a great way for anyone to start the day!

As I turn in through the electric gates, which yet again are open, I take a deep breath. I want to arrive and give a good first, well second, impression. As I pull up outside the main entrance, the same man is standing in the very same place and greets me with a very polite, "good morning Sir" and a, "welcome back to Tx3". I smile and ask, "where would you like me to park the car"? as I suddenly realise there aren't any cars hanging around. He smiles a jolly sort of smile, "leave the keys with me Sir and I will have the car collected, parked and valeted while you are here". As I walk through the main doors Annie is already walking towards me, arms open, ready to give me a big hug and kiss on the cheek. "Welcome back so soon Greg, I knew you wouldn't be able to resist the lure of the job and the anticipation of your first project", Annie announces with great confidence.

Annie then turns and directs me to follow her, "come and have a cup of tea and a catch up, I have someone I want you to meet, someone who will be giving you all the details of your first target and someone who I believe you will learn to rely on". As I make myself comfortable with a very nice cup of tea, Annie starts to explain the project they want me to be involved with. She is just getting into her stride, when a man knocks the door and walks straight in at the same time. "Hi I'm Christian", he says, as he swaggers into Annie's office. I can instantly tell Christian is a bit of a rogue, someone who doesn't like to be told what to do, or how to do it. He has no hair but has a well kept beard and clearly keeps himself fit. "So you are this Greg that I keep hearing about, welcome to the mad house at last, we've been waiting ages for you to join us". I can't tell if Christian is pleased or annoyed to be meeting me. As he walks further into the office, he smirks and continues, "unfortunately, the friggin compliance team had to carry out their so called due diligence and tick box exercises, but you're here now and that's all that matters I suppose". Annie, looking slightly uncomfortable, interjects with, "as you can see this is Christian, the person I was telling you about. Christian may appear a little unorthodox, but unfortunately he is the best in the business, so we tend to put up with his lack of manners". Christian glances at me in a cocky way, he already knows in his own mind, that he is the best and he doesn't need to be told, but he clearly likes it when it is said.

"Greg, my new assistant", he continues, "I have a project that I need you to run with and I need to bring you up to speed ASAP! We will be getting you over to the U.S immediately as I want you to make a casual introduction, nothing complicated but I would love to get the ball rolling. As we progress, I will fill you in with all the deets. You'll be gone for a few days initially, while we get you positioned. You'll be introduced to the target by a connect that we have posted there. We know this connect very well and he will make the introduction to the target that much easier. You just need to get to know them, get into their heads and hopefully after a few meetings, you can introduce Tx3. By this time you would have completed all your training, so you'll know exactly what you are doing and how to explain the benefits to the target. The bit we can't teach you is the interaction, the soft people skills, basically the stuff you already know and live and breath. After all Greg, people buy people right"? Christian is good, he knows what he is doing and has clearly been doing it a long time. "Any questions"? "I have a few, yes. Like how can I get to the US and back in a few days, the flight alone is like ten hours? Secondly how can I contact you if I need to discuss anything and finally I will need to call my wife to explain I won't be around for a few days, which will cause a few child care issues. I'm sure there will be a few more questions but that's a good start. Oh and also, have you really employed me just to sell some benefits".

Christian laughs out loud! A proper laugh, but not because I've said anything funny, but because he wants to be the alpha male in this room. He wants to make me feel uncomfortable before he answers my questions and it has worked! "Greg.. lets address your first point - you will be, how shall I say... transported to the U.S instantly. By instantly I mean we agree you are ready and then ta dah, you are there! This is all part of the clever technology that we have here at Tx3. We have been developing this stuff for years and it shouldn't need pointing out that this is all top secret, highly classified and someone will seriously kick your ass if you even think about telling anyone, including your wife". "In terms of contacting us, you can just come back any time you need to. So if you get into any sort of trouble then you can just leave, instantly and be back here straight away. I invented this whole process so trust me it works like a dream and I do mean, like a dream. You are gonna love it and you'll be blown away by it all".

The next stupid point about you speaking to your wife, I'm just going to ignore, because, if you'd been listening to Annie, you'd recall she told you that even though you'll be away for a while, you will get back here within a few seconds from the time you left. Even quicker if you run into trouble and want to activate the boomerang process. So unless the building is destroyed in the few seconds that you are away, you will be back here, almost as soon as you leave. So you can go home to your wife, kids and your lovely suburban lifestyle tonight, without any issues".

Christian is certainly asserting his alpha male role. I can tell he loves being the centre of attention and he enjoys having a new audience to play to. Rolling his eyes at Annie, "Do I even need to answer the last question? or can I leave that one to you", he sarcastically asks, like he owns the business and Annie is his personal assistant. "I'm going to start setting up so we can finally get this project moving".

The next three hours are like a whirlwind, with lots of debriefs and acronyms that didn't make any sense and constant references to the 1950's. Also plenty of training into Tx3 and how to sell the benefits to the targets. What does make sense are the instructions for the job in hand, who I have to meet, where we will meet, why this is so important, along with anything and everything they know about the target and the time period. I will need to be at my best, if I stand any chance in getting close to the target, but I feel strangely ready to start and I am eager to prove I am the right person for the job.

The team have changed my clothes so I will fit in when I arrive and as Christian tells me, "until they can trust me, they will be treating me like a child and doing all the packing for me, including my underwear"! I just agree, as it is clearly easier to do so. Once I am ready I need to be injected with my "boomerang", which is inserted in my armpit, so I can't accidentally trigger it at the wrong time. The system needs to scan my fingerprint in order to activate it and enable my safe return. What I'm not prepared for, is the incredibly sharp pain, lasting a few seconds after it's inserted. Christian clearly thinks it's funny to watch me double over in pain, while telling me, "at least you only have that done once". I'm not convinced that he's had it done, so why am I supposed to be the tough guy. I am finally ready and what's more, I actually feel ready, or maybe I just feel ready to get on with it.

I step inside a room that looks like a sci-fi film set, but this is real. I then step onto a round, slightly raised platform and nod confirmation that I am ready. The machine kicks into action, with blue lights flashing all around the edge and then immediately I find myself standing in a room with a window overlooking a park. The sun is dazzling through the window and it is clearly a beautiful hot and sunny day. Glancing at the clock, it reads eleven forty and I have to meet my connect at midday, in a coffee shop just down the road. Out of the window there are a few 1950's cars driving pass and all the people moving around are in their 1950's clothes, which of course I am also wearing. The colours seem much more vibrant than back in 2019, the green grass is popping out at me. "Holy Shit", are my first words, which are not exactly as poignant as "one small step for man, one giant leap for mankind", but it's all I have at this very moment of utter disbelief that this has worked.

Eight

I am officially a time traveller and this realisation
makes me feel awesome for it. I am so pumped and
I know I have to calm myself down, as I start my
walk to the meeting place. By the time I arrive I
am convinced I blend in perfectly and casually yet
confidently pull open the door. A young lady serves
me a hot cup of tea that I request. "Are you here on
business"? she asks, handing over my cup. I nod
and ask, "but how do you know"? "Oh", she
replies, "your British accent is adorable and you
can just tell that you are not from these parts". I
smile, "yep, you can say that again". As I find a

table, the irony that I am sitting in yet another coffee shop, slowly stirring my tea and watching others go about their business, is not lost on me. The stiff collar on my shirt irritating me as it has done since I arrived. It is all stiff and starchy, which has given me a particular itch that I can't stop. In and out walk the customers and then there's me, just sat here contemplating life and how friggin amazing it has suddenly turned out to be, in such a very short space of time. I know I have to meet my connect, a man who works here in this time and who knows the target. This man called Thomas, will be the introducer and apparently took the same trip as me several years ago, but with a different part of the Tx3 project. The plan is simply for Tom, as he likes to be called, to become a key figure in the company, building up trust ahead of my arrival. When the time is right he will receive instructions of where, when and who to meet, which of course turns out to be me. Tom will then part with as much knowledge as he can and assist where possible.

The coffee shop is bustling with people, some are mums with kids, some are retired folk, some are business people having meetings. Some are men and women just sitting by themselves waiting for someone or just taking a break, which yet again feels all too familiar. The point is, I'm not sat here with a great big sign saying, time travelling man this way, but in walks Tom, he spots me and walks straight towards me, offering his hand saying "hi, you must be Greg"? I still don't know how the hell this happens? I respond with the usual niceties, however this feels strange as I'm not fully in control this time. Tom is quick to ask about how life is, where I have come from and what technology we have at the moment. I explain mobile phones, sat nav and even iwatches and Tom is like a puppy lapping up my every word. "After all", he explains, "life is very different here in

1959". He leans towards me to speak in a quieter voice, "we think we are all modern and this is as good as it will get, but let's be frank they haven't seen The Beatles in the sixties yet, now that will blow everyone's minds". I haven't had time to think of it like that and yet Tom is spot on. "Have you seen footage of the sixties then Tom"? I ask. Tom's broad smile is from ear to ear and his eyes light up as he whispers, "no I haven't seen any footage, because I was actually there and they were the best years of my life, my time travelling life, that is. The furthest I have been allowed to travel is 1973, not enough clearance you see. The start of seventies were cool as well though, but nothing compared to the sixties in my opinion". He sits back in his chair, clearly recalling his memories, before continuing, "right now though, I live here in the fifties with my wife and three children. We have a good, honest life because of my job, we want for nothing as Tx3 take care of that and that's a great thing, but boy I love to travel. Hey your clearance must be the highest level if you can get here to me, from where you've come from! Does that mean you can also go the other way? You know, forward by fifty years or so"? Now in fairness that is a great question, although, I don't have the answer for Tom at this stage. In comparison to my usual meetings and the initial pleasantries this is on a whole new level of discussion and if I'm being honest, I like it. However, "I don't suppose we can sit here all day" I say, "so let's get down to business shall we"? Tom suddenly sits up straight and his face changes, looking focused. "Greg, I need you to meet some people in the morning, so you'll have time to think about your approach. But there is one person in particular that I need you to get close to. This person will become very influential in the future and yet their time at the top will be short. Clearly we don't want to lose this person or their contacts and knowledge, so we need to start the process now. From tomorrow onwards we need you to start getting close to him, build up his trust while he gets to know you. This is simply about you being yourself, your 1950's self of course and the rest will all fall into place, I'm sure".

Tom sips his tea, then continues, "I will meet you back here, tomorrow morning at nine thirty ready for our meeting at ten. In the meantime here is everything that I know about the target, but don't open it here, take it back to your place so you can read through it properly. You can read everything and the planned approach. We can then turn up tomorrow ready to make our approach". I thank Tom and as weird as it sounds, I feel like we could become great friends. Maybe it's because he is my only friend in this time, but maybe it's because we have simply connected.

As I arrive back at my place, I appreciate how simple life is, here in the glorious fifties. This is the type of place where I could enjoy a lovely peaceful holiday. How ridiculous does that sound? Imagine me at home, saying to Bonnie, "hey I have found the perfect holiday destination so I've booked us two weeks in the fifties"! Crazy, but it is just a wonderfully uncomplicated place to be.

These days, as soon as we walk into someone's house the twins are asking for the Wi-Fi codes to connect their various gadgets. The TVs are on, mobile devices are never, ever, turned off and we are always at the beck and call of clients, who by the way want answers immediately. Gone are the days, or so I thought, where a query would be raised and we'd write a letter and you'd get a reply a few weeks later. Now an email arrives and ten minutes later the same person is ringing to chase for an answer. However, here in the fifties, life appears to be the exact opposite! No email, no internet, no pressure to deliver immediately, just a calm destination. Maybe I should write the travel advert for it?

After a light meal, I sit down to read the file and get to know my target. After all I need to be prepared, this is my first assignment and I would love to return home being successful. As I open the file, I am drawn to a photo clipped to the inside cover. The photo is of a handsome young man, with bright green eyes, staring back at me. Written above his photo : John Dickson, up and coming influential business man. I am incredibly impressed with how he has progressed from small town boy, to the head of a decent size business. On paper he is living the American dream and his life couldn't be any rosier. Having read the whole report, I am disappointed as there isn't anything that really stands out. I am here, a time traveller, a spy (in my mind anyway) and yet I am to attend a meeting, to talk to the same type of people as I always have. The only difference being, it is in the fifties and my bank balance is a lot healthier than it has ever been. I don't need to get the sale done quickly, I just need to go to the meetings, go through the steps and make sure we get there in the end. It can and probably will, take time, but in reality I am not using up any of my real life time, so it doesn't matter. The icing on the cake of course, is that I don't have to do any of the boring paperwork.

Nine

The following morning, shortly after breakfast I head back to the coffee shop to meet my new friend Tom. I guess he is more a colleague than a friend though and I arrive just before nine thirty as agreed. This time Tom is already waiting for me, which makes things a whole lot easier. "Morning Tom", I announce all chipper, as I approach the table. Tom seems just as pleased to see me as yesterday, "morning, how'd you sleep", is his reply as we enter the small talk part of any good meeting. Once we're done with the chit chat, Tom gets straight down to business. "So here is how it will work, we need you to go in and do your thing, sell our company and once you have the in, we can then build on the relationship from there. In terms of any of the actual work, I can take care of that back in the office. Your sole focus needs to be on getting close to John". Smiling at Tom, trying my best not to be condescending, I ask, "exactly how many meetings have you had with this John? After all we are not just going to walk in there for the first time and sell something straight away, that's not how this works", I tell him. Tom looks at me, looking slightly embarrassed and nods his head, "i've not actually met John face to face before". "Bingo, you've been doing it all wrong then haven't you". Tom's embarrassed face turns into a big smile, "wow, that's why they drafted you in then".

We arrive at Johns office a few minutes before the meeting. Tom wants to wait until ten, on the dot, before entering the building. Following a brief discussion, Tom agrees that from now on, I will be the boss and he will do whatever I say. He seems to like this, as it means he doesn't have to think, only do. We enter the building and straight into the reception area. As I glance around there is a young lady at a desk typing, who has clearly been crying this morning, but is doing her best to keep it together. The other side is another very well dressed lady, who has a sign in front of her stating "reception", which is clearly where we need to walk towards. "Good morning" I start, "we have a meeting with Mr John Dickson", handing her my business card, which Tom provided in the file yesterday. "The meeting is arranged for ten" I say smiling, while turning around to survey the rest of the office. The lady calls through to Mr Dickson, to announce our arrival and quickly replies with, "Mr Dickson will be with you shortly". A few minutes later John Dickson arrives, with his hand out ready to shake mine. He is as handsome as his photo and we dutifully enter his office, as directed.

"Thank you for your time today, Mr Dickson", I start with. This is always a great opening line as it makes the person feel superior to you, because it gives the impression that their time is far more important than your own. I quickly follow up with "and it's such a lovely day out there, don't you think"? Then comes a quick and direct reply, "please call me John, Mr Dickson always makes me feel old", I agree and also suggest putting "uncle" in front of the name does the same thing! A few pleasantries in and I can see that John is already trying to move the meeting along. He is clearly a genuinely busy man, to which he eventually states, "time is short today I'm afraid chaps, so let's get down to business, why exactly are you here"? I proceed to explain, "we have been asked to review your current arrangements to see if we can offer you something more competitive. Personally, I want to ensure the product is better as well as you getting a cost benefit". However, I can sense we are about to be given short thrift with this tack. So I change direction slightly, "although, I don't want to talk to you about any of this today". Well, Tom's head almost falls off as he spins around so quickly and even John stops writing on his pad to look up. "Well, why the hell are you here then"? Is John's aggressive response. "Look", I start, smiling at the same time, "we can't even begin to talk to you about a potential solution, unless we know exactly how you operate, being truthful we don't really know anything about your business and we would be lying if we said otherwise. Yes we know who you are, we know your position in this company, but we don't really know anything else. We would like to spend a few days with you, understanding what it is you really do, how you do it and only then can we have a discussion about how we might be able to help your business going forwards. That is why I'm confident we can find a solution tailored to your needs. Today however is simply about meeting you, asking a few questions and starting that process. By the end John, I'm confident we will be close friends, that have your best interests at heart".

John smiles at me, leans back in his chair and looks at us, with a long pause. Tom is about to speak to break up the awkward silence, so I gently tap his leg, and gesture a no, with my finger. This is the big moment of the meeting and we do not want to be the first ones to speak. After a fairly long pause, John's response finally comes, "of all the meetings I've had, that is the most refreshing and honest thing I've heard. Do you know what Greg, I think you and me are going to get along just fine". I'm pleased that I read the meeting well and quickly follow up with, "why don't we have lunch together in a few days time, so we can get to know each other a bit better"? John accepts and confirms, "I will get my secretary to contact you to arrange it all".

We were in and out of the meeting in under twenty minutes, we hadn't obtained any information and we certainly didn't sell, or even attempt to sell anything and yet Tom is like a puppy bouncing around. "That was brilliant" is all he can keep saying, "that went swimmingly". From my perspective it was job done, for meeting one. Now I can have a few days to relax and sightsee, so a win, win really.

A few days later I meet John for lunch and really get to know each other, or more realistically, I get to know John a lot better. He is a driven man, who, if he keeps going at the pace he is, will end up having a heart attack or something, but he is a nice man with a good heart. Right at the end of our night and after quite a few drinks, John starts to properly relax. He starts talking about his staff and one young lady in particular, called Marion, who is the filing clerk, who was in the office the other day. I honestly thought he was going to tell me about how he'd tried it on with her, but I was wrong. He actually says, "she started out being very good at her job and I thought she might progress to receptionist and beyond, at some point. However, things appear to have changed recently and now I'm thinking she'll have to be fired". He looks genuinely upset with this, "life is tough I guess" are his exact words and "maybe she just can't hack it anymore". John shakes his head and I sit listening, conscious not to judge too early. John continues, "or maybe she's met a young fella and she's thinking of getting married, so thinks she won't need the job anymore. Who knows, either way I guess she needs to be let go".

I sip my drink, making sure he has finished talking, before I gently question, "can I suggest another approach John"? "Why yes of course, not that it'll make any difference though", John acknowledges. I look him straight in the eye, "can I suggest that before you fire her, you ask her what is happening at home"? John's face scrunches at me and John appears confused, so I continue, "you need to ask her why she is coming into work upset and then you can offer to help, if it's at all possible"?

John looks at me, even more confused now! "Why would anything be wrong, how do you know she's coming into work upset. How the hell can I help her and what's that got to do with her work"? I make sure to smile a friendly smile at John, "that's a lot of questions in one go, but John you see, if she is having problems at home, then it is clearly affecting her work. So if you can understand what the problem is, you might be able to help her out and then she will be back working at full speed again, as good as she used to. You won't need to fire her, or train someone else up either". After a few more drinks we decide to call it a night, but not before John agrees to give my approach with Marion a go. "I'm still not convinced" he keeps saying, "but I'll give it a go, I promise". I'm genuinely pleased, "Good, I will pop by your office on Monday afternoon, to see how you are getting on". For me this is perfect, as I get to see John again next week and I can keep everything nicely on track.

I have a very relaxed weekend, with lots of sleep, a bit of reading and some sightseeing which is a welcome change to my normal weekends at home. I now feel ready and raring to go again. Monday means another trip to see John, to keep getting close to him and to see if my ideas with Marion have worked. If they have, then John is sure to trust me a little more, which is a good step towards introducing the concept of Tx3.

Today is another sunny day, here in the fifties U.S.A. A bird chirping, children laughing in the park, kind of day. I feel reenergised and chipper and if I'm being honest, I can't remember the last time I felt like this and I love it! A thought suddenly flashes through my mind, am I really getting paid a ridiculous amount of money to meet people, build relationships and effectively have a holiday, all at the same time? This is strange and yet wonderful at the same time. If it stays like this, when I get home I will be fully recharged and ready to go about my hectic life once again, in the knowledge I can escape again when I need to to.

I decide to mooch around the town for a few hours, soaking up the atmosphere, until two in the afternoon. As the local town hall clock strikes two, I start to stroll, in the warm sunshine, towards John's office. As I approach, I'm not too sure what I am walking into today. With slight trepidation I open the main door and am greeted with smiles, from everyone, including Marion, who looks ten times happier than she was the last time I was here. As I close the door behind me, I hear a happy, "welcome young man" booming from the office at the rear, as John walks to meet me. "Get in here", he playfully shouts, slapping me on the back, as I enter his domain. "What a night we had last week eh", he says, closing his office door. Then, as soon as the door clicks shut, John immediately reduces his speech to a much quieter tone, "you were absolutely right about Marion! How'd you know? No don't tell me, it doesn't matter, but what you need to know, is that there are indeed problems at home with her Pa". John looks strangely happy at the fact Marion is having problems at home. It isn't anything malicious, he is just pleased he is able to help, as he explains, "following a chat and a few tears, she explained everything to me and we've agreed she can start work a bit later for the next few weeks. Marion is over the moon and apparently I'm the best boss ever". I try not to look too smug, but it feels great to make a difference to someone's life and it clearly puts me in a favourable position with John.

I stay for about forty minutes, then make my excuses, as John clearly has quite a bit going on. As I'm leaving I ask, "can you meet me for a drink this evening, I have something I would like to speak to you about". I'm relieved to hear John can meet up later and as I leave the building, I very nearly jump in the air, clicking my heels. I feel like my mojo is back, the old me returning and I am convinced Annie will be impressed with me as well.

Ten

Later that evening, with the music box playing some classic tunes, I shower, dress, change my shirt twice and brush my teeth. It's just like I'm heading out on a big date, back, or is that forwards, in the nineties. I recall the pretty brief training I'd had, just in case I find myself at this stage, but my confidence is high and I'm convinced I can carry this off. I meander into a quirky bar that we'd agreed and sit down at a corner table. I settle myself in for a spot of people watching, with a drink in hand and I feel right at home. This after all is my usual type of meeting place, whether it be a coffee shop or a bar, it doesn't matter to me, I am in my element. People come and go, some are meeting friends and one is even chatting about business, which is all very familiar to me. Then, right on time John walks into the bar, smiling at a few people and shaking hands with a man, before heading my way. John feels just like an old friend, like I've known him for years, which is a strange and yet comforting feeling. We sit and chat about Marion for a while and how she appears to be back to her high standards of work already. John tells me how they have a plan in place, which seems to suit everyone. Then the usual pause presents itself, the part where the niceties end and the person sat opposite, wants to get down to business. I smile, trying to appear calm, "so John... I guess you want to know why I asked you here"? John smirks right back at me, which makes me feel even more confident. The smirk says to me, I know exactly what you want from me, but in reality he has absolutely no idea what is coming. John gets comfy in his chair, "look... I appreciate we've gotten quite close recently and you've strangely sorted out my staffing problems, but are you really sure you are ready to handle an order as big as ours, I mean we a very demanding business? After all there are some quite complex areas and they need a great deal of attention". I calmly lean forwards, "John, we have got to know each other pretty well recently and I've always been honest with you, so let's continue in this way. My company really wants your business and I know we will do a better job than your current arrangements, however, I don't want to handle it for you". John looks wounded, and very put out, after all why wouldn't I want to look after his business. It didn't matter if he was going to give us his business or not, the atmosphere has changed. "Let me clarify that statement", I continue, "I wouldn't be the best person to run your account. I'm pretty good at the high level stuff, but I'm not a details man, a cross the T's and dot the I's sort of man. The right approach is for Tom to look after you, day to day I mean. He would give his right arm to have your account, he knows the products inside and out and it will elevate him within in the company. This means he will work so hard to keep you happy, you can have every confidence he is doing everything he needs to do for you. I want to carry on working with you as well. I can keep an eye on everything for you, but when we meet we can talk about the important things in life, without the distractions of paperwork and money, what do you think"? John once again, appears to like my directness. Following a few more drinks John agrees to appoint Tom, first thing in the morning. I am over the moon for Tom and this will certainly make his life, here in the fifties, even easier for him.

With the business side of things out of the way and a few more drinks gone, I move the conversation towards the real reason for meeting : Time. "So

John, tell me", I start, while taking a sip of my drink, "tell me what you think is the most valuable thing in the World right now. Then tell me what you think will be the most valuable thing, in the future"? John grins, "did you really bring me here to play a game"? My confidence is high, "John, the business element is a very small piece of the jigsaw, of why I'm here. I think we have enough trust between us now to talk openly and honestly about a much more important issue, so please, just humour me"? John, slightly confused agrees, but it's clear John doesn't suffer fools gladly. "Oil", is his first answer, "or gold I suppose is the most valuable thing right now, or maybe real estate, am I right with one of those"? "In a way you are right John, all of those things are incredibly valuable right now and can make a person incredibly rich. The problem is that if you work at a company that controls those things, then you will be forever trying to keep ahead of the game and of course the competition. Now suppose you make millions of dollars from one of these things, do you think you'll be happy"? John stares straight at me, "of course I'd be happy, I'd be rich, I wouldn't have to worry about anything again". I challenge straight back with, "I'm not so sure, you'll have a lot of responsibility, you'll be working very long days, every day of the week maybe and you will probably put yourself into an early grave". This leads me to my next point, while John is thinking, "how much time do you think you will have with your family, or how much time will you have for yourself"? John reluctantly agrees with me, but feels the benefits still outweigh the problems. "The challenge is to find more time John, more time to be alive, to spend it with the people we love, so we can actually enjoy life to its fullest. If we are always trying to buy the latest things, we have to constantly chase more and more money to pay for them, meaning less and less time is actually spent with the people we want to be with. I no longer want or even need to buy things, like the latest car as an example. What I want is to have more time with my loved ones, Time therefore, is the most valuable thing right now. Wouldn't it be amazing if we could pause time, or if we can find a way to harness the power of time? If we can achieve this, we can retain some brilliant people and keep their brilliant minds alive after their so called death. In doing so that would be worth more than gold, or oil put together". "I agree with you" states John, now very much alert to this conversation, "but let's get real for a moment, this is not even possible, unless of course you believe in God and heaven"! "Ahh but you miss the point", I challenge once again, "if there is a heaven and you do go there when you die, you've already left your family, friends and your life behind you and you can no longer contribute to society, so the talent of the person, whatever it may be, is then lost forever".

"Agreed", nods John, "but how is this possible and who is going to make this magic time capturing thing happen. Let's be honest here's, it's simply not possible. I'm no expert but I don't think the U.S government, USSR, or even China, have that sort of technology today, to even get started". I'm enjoying this and getting into my stride, "aha, but who says it would need to be built right now, after all it could be built in the future. There will come a day John, when we will put a man on the moon, right now no one believes this is even possible, but it will happen". John looks very intrigued, "Ok, Greg, let's assume you are not too drunk, or mad. Let's assume what you are telling me is true, why would you be telling someone like me, I can't afford to buy into a project like this and I don't think I can contribute to it either"? I smile and whisper, "in terms of cost, that's simple, it won't cost you a dime John. In terms of your second point, the World has lost many great people along with their minds and ideas, like Albert Einstein a few years back. So imagine what we lost that day. Yes we still have his teachings, but wouldn't it be amazing if he could carry on with his work, after his so called death? Do you think that if he could keep going, his ideas could continue to change the World. Now I realise not everyone can be Einstein, but there are others that have an important role to play in the future and you John, are one of them. So in simple terms, the World can't afford for you not to be a part of it in the future. You are destined for great things in the next few years and we simply can't afford to lose you and your ideas. Einstein, by the way, was already signed up, I'm pleased to tell you, so we didn't lose his incredible talent. You would be amazed if I tell you what he has gone on to achieve in the future years, but of course he cannot take any recognition, as, to the rest of the World he died. More importantly though, he has helped to literally save millions of people, by continuing his work and that is such a special thing"!

John looks completely overwhelmed and exhausted by this conversation, so I know I'm getting through to him. "I just need to know that when your time comes John, you have signed up, so we can welcome you in. After that of course, you'll be around to help continue our work with us, which will help save countless lives. I appreciate this all sounds far fetched and unrealistic but trust me, you need to be a part of this". John looks like he might burst, so I tell him not to tell anyone about this conversation. John, wide eyed, whispers a little loudly, back at me, "trust me Greg, I won't be telling anyone about any of this, or they'll think I'm in need of the asylum". "John, please have a think about everything I've said, let's meet up in a few days time, to continue this conversation and to answer any questions that you are sure to have. After that, I will need you to indicate if you are interested enough for me to get my people in touch with you. This is an exciting project and one I believe you'll want to be part of, after all you've nothing to lose and everything to gain. I'm going to head off now and leave you with your thoughts and I will get in touch in a few days time. If you want to meet before then, you'll be speaking with Tom anyway and he will know where to find me. Goodnight John and see you soon".

With that I grab my coat and hat and stand up to leave. A quick glance back at John shows he hasn't moved. It's as if he is still looking at me across the table, eyes wide and mouth open. I pat him on the shoulder and leave, like some actor in a movie swanning out and it feels great!

Eleven

As I awake in my apartment the sun is beaming
through the thin curtains, which is relaxing. I have
nowhere to go, no one to see and it feels like the
second week of a good holiday. It always takes me
the first week to unwind and to switch my work
brain off. Then as I start the second week of my
break, I usually sleep very well and my energy
levels return. Well, this is how I feel this morning,
I'm relaxed and hungry and I am able to move
around at my own pace. This is definitely the best
job ever and once I get John all signed up, then I
can go back home, to be with Bonnie and the

twins. What a great way for me to go back home, feeling refreshed and able to do more of the house things, not the usual stressed out person I've become. I won't need to rush off to a meeting, or be late home, ever again. I can cook a meal for us all, so when Bonnie walks through the door, she can enter a calm household as I'm dishing up the meal. This job is fixing all of my problems in life and it is fixing me as well.

I slip into a holiday routine a bit quickly and easily, for a few days. Late breakfast, a stroll along the beach, followed by a drink on the way back to my apartment late in the afternoon. Evenings are quiet, with some food, the radio playing and plenty of time to just breath and think. I can't remember the last time I've be on my own and not rushing to or from a meeting. However I do know that this is coming to an end shortly. Like any good holiday, towards the end you start thinking about heading back home. I am missing Bonnie and the twins, the mess they cause and surprisingly I am missing the running around I do, from one club to another. For them, I've been in work for the day, just like normal. For me though, I am determined to return a newer, happier, healthier me. I am looking forward to showing them that I can be the best dad and husband there is. This starts a feeling that drives me on, I need to get another meeting with John arranged. Hopefully he will agree to signing up to Tx3 and I can be out of here. As lovely as it is here in the fifties, it is definitely time for me to head home.

I decide to take some action and stroll around to Johns office, on the off chance he will see me, or at least agree to meet up later. John I'm pleased to say, welcomes me with open arms and a nice friendly smile. "What took you so long", he asks, as I enter his office. "How have you been", I enquire. John starts telling me about how Tom has been working very hard following his appointment and he feels confident they have done the right thing. Then John just stops, looks at me and pulls up a chair next to me. "Tell me, we did have a strange conversation the other night didn't we? I mean it was real, right"? I simply nod my head but I don't open my mouth, before John carries on with, "thank God for that, I was wondering if I was going mad. I've replayed it over and over in my mind and came to the conclusion we might have been very drunk, or worse, I'd somehow taken LSD. At least I know it's real, thank you. I have to say though, that no matter how many times I've replayed the conversation in my head, I always come back to the same question. You said I might have a few questions, but I only have the one : why me? Why have you approached me? After all I'm no Einstein as your example". John looks emotionally drained, which I have not seen in him before and it is endearing. I simply smile a warm friendly smile at him, "John you may not know why... yet... but trust me, the World cannot afford to lose you and what you will become over the next few years. I can't tell you anymore than that or I could reshape history and defeat the whole purpose of my visit with you. I have read all about you in the history books and it is an honour to meet you. Please, just live your life, taking the opportunities as they arise and you will discover that life can be very unexpected as indeed death, or supposed death, can be as well. I work for a company called Tx3 and they want you to sign up to our exciting project to protect you in the future, which will also help to protect our future generations. You have nothing to lose but everything to gain. What do you say John? Are you in"?

John leans right back in his chair, visibly shaking, then turns to me, with his steely green eyes and confirms, "yes, I'm in". I feel quite emotional, which catches me by surprise, "fantastic news" I manage to get out of my dry mouth, "it will be an honour to meet you again in the future, as I'm sure we will do. I will get everything set up by the team and you will receive a visit shortly. The team will introduce themselves by stating they are from Tx3 and remember this cannot be discussed with anyone, ever"! John agrees and looks exhausted, I almost want to give him a hug and tell him it will all be okay. Instead I stand, smile and offer my hand. "Good luck John" I announce all professionally, "we will meet again". John glances up at me, looking grateful, just in time to see me pressing my boomerang.

Christian is still sat in his chair, staring at me as I stand there looking back at him. I feel like I'm in shock, I feel emotional, it's relief I suppose, after all I have completed my first mission and it has all gone to plan. I feel a sense of pride as well. I now feel a worthy member of the team, it's almost as if my shoulders have grown wider. Christian, stands and as he starts to walk towards me, smirking, he states, "it's a rush, isn't it? It's a mind bending, brilliant machine! How'd you get on"? He continues, "I'm assuming you got the job done? Right? Or you wouldn't have had the balls to come back". I nod, "yes all done and John is onboard". Christian looks more relieved than pleased but is still able to say, "Fantastic and well done", which I appreciate, "we will send in our repat team next, so we can finalise the agreement with John". I feel more achievement from this one job than I have from the last few years of work. Christian explains, "we need to finalise a few of the deets today, but we can welcome him to Tx3 tomorrow".

"Tomorrow"? I shout a little too loud, at Christian, without thinking first, "tomorrow, why so fast, I thought he would go on to achieve great things, live a decent life and then get brought in"?

Christian, laughs at me, a proper smug laugh! "Greg, you have not learned anything yet, have you? It will be tomorrow for us, once my brilliant self gets everything sorted of course, but for John it will be 1978, the day he dies. As this is history, we know exactly what time and day he dies, we just need to be there and as it's in the past, it means he can arrive here tomorrow! Not that you'll need to get involved in any of these next steps, your role is done and Tx3 thanks you. Now go home, enjoy your wife and family for a while and I will see you when we discuss your next target". This all feels a bit final, like I'm no longer needed. "By the way" Christian starts again, "get plenty of rest as we've already lined up your next target, it will be another John. This next one though, will be a lot harder, so you will need lots strength". As condescending as Christian can be, I actually do need to go home and see everyone, it has been ages, well ages for me anyway. As I head to the cool down room, to shower and change, I shout over my shoulder to Christian, "so what time can we expect John to arrive tomorrow"? Christian looks like he has it all planned out already and confirms, "eleven thirty seven, to be precise, just before lunch, although John probably won't want anything to eat when he arrives, as he will be in a bit of shock. We will have councillors waiting for him along with a team of people who can help him. He will be transported to the S.H where he can relax for a few days, acclimatise to his new life before we can show him how he can help us. All planned, nothing for you to do, so you can bugger off home knowing it's taken care of". As Christian turns back to his systems, I shout back, "just one more question if I may? What the friggin hell is S.H"? Christian doesn't even turn back, like it's just wasting too much energy and I can tell he is frustrated with me, as he replies in a very sarcastic way - "Safe Haven, obviously".

I quickly shower and change ready for my drive home. That was certainly one long day at work, I chuckle to myself. Once I am refreshed I head to my office, which Annie made sure has a great view of the rear of the property and boy do I feel like the cat that got the cream. Big office, large comfy chairs, great pc and screen, but as I'm sat here looking around at everything, I do wonder if I will ever use any of them. I mean, my job is clearly for me to be anywhere other than in my office, yet this is an amazing set up, and it feels a bit weird, having an actual office. Annie enters, with a polite and quiet knock on the glass door along with a very big smile on her face. "Congratulations on a very successful first assignment", Annie proudly announces. "Did you enjoy it"? I am beaming from ear to ear and can't hide my pride and neither do I want to. "Yes" I burst out, "it was fantastic, it took a couple of weeks to get it all sorted, but I'm very pleased it all worked out in the end". I continue, "Christian tells me John will be with us tomorrow, which is amazing and I guess exciting for the next stage". Annie also looks relieved, as she confirms, "this one successful mission means hundreds of thousands of people should now benefit from his arrival. We are praying he will be able to settle in and start work quite quickly, on a particular project the government set up about two years ago. His arrival is the perfect timing to take the project to the next level, as the current team have gone as far as they can and everyone is convinced John has what is needed to move it forwards again. I'm actually convinced he will thoroughly enjoy this challenge as well. Anyway Greg, I bet you're eager to get home to your family, who you haven't seen for at least"... Annie glances at her watch, then smirks at me, then looking back at me, finishes with, "for at least a few hours"! I fully appreciate her humour and I have to admit, that I am eager to get home to my family. I am looking forward to the drive home and I feel like a winner again, like I've made a difference for once. I stroll, broad shouldered to the front of the building, where my beautiful, shiny car is sat waiting for me, like a dutiful pet. I climb into the plush driving seat, pull on my sun glasses and gently squeeze the loud pedal, which makes me tingle with excitement.

As I head home, I have time to think about my family and how this job will help bring stability for everyone. The twins will have their dad home a lot more and I will certainly have more energy and more importantly, a lot less stress, which has to be a good thing. As I arrive on the driveway looking at my beautiful home, I am grateful to be back. I walk towards the house, I ready myself for the noise and the chaos that happens nearly every time I push the door open. This time feels different though, I feel much more grounded and centred, not exhausted and stressed from the day. I open the door and immediately the chaos engulfs me and it feels simply wonderful. Bonnie is cooking food, the twins are changing themselves into their football kits and everything looks normal, which I guess it is to them. I have been away for days, but to them it was just a normal day. I smile at Bonnie and let her know that I will finish getting them ready. I don't have any work calls to make or receive, so I can give them one hundred percent of my attention. Bonnie looks at me, half a smile, but with a look of thank goodness for that. As she stands up, she confirms, "the food is pretty much ready, you only need to plate it up and the twins need to be at training in an hour". Bonnie looks exhausted, so I suggest she "go and have a shower, have some food while we are out and we can catch up later". Bonnie clearly doesn't need telling twice as she is already trudging up the stairs, as I head to the kitchen to see what I need to plate up.

The evening goes easily enough with the twins running around in the evening air, with their team mates and coaches. All I have to do is stand in between the two pitches, with one eye on each side watching and cheering occasionally. I chat to a couple of the other parents and listen to the crap day they've had. The traffic, the meetings, the stress appears to be the same for everyone, everyone that is, except me, but I play along anyway. Deep down I feel content I suppose. We arrive back home around bedtime for the twins and Bonnie is nowhere to be seen. The twins ask after her and I tell them, "mum has gone to bed early as she'd had a very busy day". Before I get them off to bed, we sit on the sofa and watch some TV for a while. They chat about an idiot boy in school and for the first time in ages, I am actually here with them. I don't mean physically, I mean I am actually engaged in the conversation and I am not distracted by work, whizzing around my brain. It feels wonderful and I'm convinced they actually look a bit older, for some reason. It is like I am seeing and hearing them for the first time in ages and it is a great end to the day for me. Soon enough the twins are tucked up in their beds with night lights on and the house begins to breath quietly after its manic day. I sneak back downstairs into the silence, ready to do battle with the kitchen mess and then tidy the main room from the clothes which look like they've been thrown everywhere. My goal is to clear it all now, so we can be ready for a clean start in the morning. Then I can sit down with a nice cold beer before bed. The house is suddenly very quiet and calm and it is a wonderful time to be alone to relax. I start to make plans in my head, holiday plans, as I am sure Bonnie needs a break now more than ever and before she burns herself out completely. We have the money now to go on a great holiday, but of course Bonnie isn't even aware of how much money I, or should I say we, have. In the morning I need to talk to her about us taking a break and I think it will be good for us all. Of course I need to ask Bonnie where she would like us to go. Can we go soon, will be the next hurdle, but nothing we can't resolve, if we get organised. I too trundle off to bed, tired from the day, but not as battered as I would normally have been. Bonnie is already fast asleep, curled up in the bed covers and clearly does not want to be disturbed, so I climb in quietly and drift off to sleep.

The alarm wakes us, like it does every morning and Bonnie and myself clamber out of bed, to start yet another marathon day of work, kids and life. I head downstairs to get things started and leave Bonnie to it. As she enters the kitchen half an hour later, I have breakfast ready with a nice cup of tea. The laptop is open on the holiday pages, ready for Bonnie to look and have a chat, before work. As she walks in, I sit her down, all excited to talk about where and when we can all get away together. Bonnie immediately shoots me down though, "how do you expect us to take time off right now? I am very busy on a project in work and if you have been listening you would know that. Also you've only just started a new job, so its not like you can have time off straight away is it"? Bonnie is clearly angry with me for even suggesting it. I try to explain I can have as much time off as I want, which provokes Bonnie's anger to another level. "Listen to what you are saying", she screams at me, "do you really expect me to believe you have a job where you can take as much time off as you want, don't make me out to be an idiot! And before you even think of answering that, what about the twins, or have you forgotten we have young children that are in school right now… today in fact. You can't just take them out of school whenever you please, or whenever you fancy taking some time off. This is all about you as usual, isn't it? You have probably started this new job, which by the way you haven't even bothered telling me anything about, its like you think I'm a mind reader or something and the job hasn't turned out to be what you expected. So as usual you have jumped into another job, purely for the money and not a thought about how this will affect your family. I bet you hated the job yesterday and now you're trying to get out of there". I just stand frozen, in the middle of the kitchen, mouth wide open, anger pulsing through my body and trying to hold it all together - where did that come from? The only thing I can say, is, "actually I had a really good day in the new job yesterday and I think this will be the best thing I have done, the best move I have ever made in terms of work and" … but Bonnie immediately jumps in, shouting, "well that's what you would say isn't it? You wouldn't exactly admit you've made a mistake now would you"? I am angry of course, but I am more confused than ever. Yet again I am trying to do the right thing for the family and yet again I end up looking like the evil, bad guy that is plotting against the rest of them. Bonnie, didn't even look at the holiday page, let alone eat her breakfast or drink her tea. She is up and out the front door quicker than a burglar, with the alarm blaring. I am still standing in the kitchen, shaking with anger and shock, muttering to myself, like some sort of idiotic man. So I do the only sensible thing I can do and that is to go and wake up the twins. I need to get them up and ready for school, so we can all just get on with our day. As I climb the stairs I make up my mind to go into work again today, rather than hang around the house driving myself mad. I can welcome John, as he arrives at what will probably be a very difficult and stressful time for him. At least in doing this, I will be useful, rather than staying at home, getting more and more annoyed with what has happened this morning.

Twelve

Arriving at work, feels very normal, which in itself is not normal. I have already worked on my target for a few weeks, but in reality this is only my second day on the job. I am still fuming from this morning's Bonnie Bashing session, but I don't want to show it. So like all the other times before, no matter where I'm working, I turn up with a big smile on my face, crack a few jokes and pretend everything is just sweet as a nut. I know the routine now, drop off the car, leave the keys, enter the main area and then I head to my office, like I have been going to and from this office for years. I pass a few people and say, "good morning", in a very happy tone, like I know them very well. Although in reality I don't know them at all, let alone recognise them, so perhaps we have never even seen each other, but it makes me feel welcome here and better about myself. I am determined to have a good day today, regardless of how it started. No sooner have I arrived, Christian bursts through the door. "Morning", he says sarcastically, looking at his watch, because it is clearly not very early in the morning. "Guess you can't stay away from this place"? I smile a forced smile back and ask, "is John still arriving at eleven thirty seven as planned"? Christian looks at me, like I have two heads, "Of course he is, I have it all planned out"! So I quickly calculate we have about forty five minutes until John gets here. "So how does this work"? I ask. Christian loves it when he knows all the answers and I am clearly the novice here. "This is the fun part", he states, "the systems are all set up and we have been tracking him since you were with him back in the fifties. The exact split second he dies, the boomerang system is activated and pulls him from the scene, his "actual" body will remain there, so no one knows any difference, his "spirit" body for want of a better phrase, will arrive here immediately after. John and all our targets, only feel a sharp and very quick pin prick, as the homing device is activated at the exact moment they are dying, a bit like giving blood at the hospital. However, this is instantly forgotten about, when they look around and see our gormless faces staring back at them. Then, we usually have a slight pause while their brains try and comprehend the fact they are not dead. Next, relief kicks in that what they were told by someone like you, is actually true. I have spoken with many of the targets about the transfer experience and they all say they had a small amount of doubt, that when the time came, this might not work. Human nature I guess! It is an incredible feeling to be part of this project, but never more so than at that very moment".

I am starting to feel a bit anxious and yet excited for John's arrival. Will he even recognise me? Will he be relived like Christian said? Or will he be angry, upset and emotional? I guess I will find out shortly, but realise I am more anxious than excited. As the time approaches I stroll to the main room, my legs are slightly heavy and wobbly. I can't really understand my feelings, after all, I'm not the one dying today. Just as Christian had said, there are people stood around the room, waiting for John's arrival. A few faces I recognise but the majority I don't. There are a few in white coats, as if they are medical experts and I wonder if they are on hand in case something goes wrong. I start to get fidgety, hot even and I wonder if I will faint, which will be a terrible inconvenience to the team, who need to focus on John. All the faces are staring at an empty area in the middle of the room and I notice everyone looks completely calm, which is clearly the opposite to myself. I guess these are the experts after all and they have probably been here a few times before. Suddenly a loud klaxon sounds and a computer voice alerts everyone to John's imminent arrival. The lights dim and turn to a red / blue calming colour, which makes it even more theatrical. I can feel my heart pumping out of my chest, I am hardly breathing but am determined not to miss this moment. I suddenly feel like a child at Christmas, waiting in the crowd to see Santa and I don't want to miss one second of it. Ten seconds the computer voice announces and the whole team, like a well rehearsed army, ready themselves, clipboards, pens and doctors stethoscopes all at the ready. I think I should ready myself as well with something, but I have nothing to offer at this exact moment. I steady myself, by shuffling my feet then planting them firmly to the ground, like a soldier at ease. Five seconds, booms out of the speakers again, four seconds, three seconds, two seconds, one second... then there is a very weird noise and a sort of low brightness type flash and John is standing right in front of me, although facing Christian on the other side of the room. John however is now visibly older, I can't see his face but it is obvious he had aged since I saw him yesterday.

The room remains deadly silent, it's like time has literally stopped, I glance around the room and nobody seems to be moving. Maybe I'm the one that has died? It is an incredibly surreal moment and I have nothing to compare this with. Then, exactly as Christian said, John just stands there, frozen for a second or two, which feels like an awful lot longer. But suddenly, from out of no where, John screams at the top of his voice, "Oh My God it worked. It actually worked", quickly followed by a very loud laugh, not of happiness but a scared and relieved type of laugh.

John starts to move his head, slowly at first, then the rest of his body. He looks around the room at the faces, trying to recognise any of them that are now moving towards him to help. He eventually turns so far around that our eyes meet and he gives me the most amazing smile I have ever seen from anyone. An angelic, almost other worldly smile. I can feel his warmth radiate through my body instantly and we haven't even touched. I realise I am moving quickly towards him, involuntary movement, but moving all the same. John ignores all the experts who are here to help him and he heads straight to me. We instantly embrace, with a full on man hug, a big slap on the back man type of hug. John grabs at my face with both of his hands and he has a beaming smile, from ear to ear. "Friggin hell you haven't aged a bit, since the last time I saw you", he says shakily. "I haven't seen you in about twenty five years or so I guess? Wow you are like some kind of Peter Pan or something". John scrunching his forehead in a confused way, mumbles to himself, "how is that even possible"? I try to find the right words, but struggle, to eventually say, "it's just great to see you again" and then, my mind goes blank again, I can't think of anything else, other than, "Welcome to your new life". John looks strangely healthy and not like you'd expect a dead man to look, at all. He is however, pulled away from me, by the others, so they can check him over. He is however quickly able to say, "thank you, thank you for being here to meet me today, it means everything to me".

I realise in this very moment, that if I ever have the honour of getting to this stage again, I will make sure I am here for their arrival. It clearly makes a big difference to John and it has made a huge difference to me. In this moment I feel complete, I feel like I've seen the job through to the end and I feel like I have achieved something. I want to feel wanted in life, I'm the sort of person that likes to be liked and this project with John has helped me, to start finding myself again. I now feel a part of a team and its success and I've learned to relax a little and to start enjoying life once again. I know I have a long way to go, to rid myself of decades of stress, but in this particular moment, I feel like I have made big strides towards that. As I stand here in my warm glow, watching everyone frantically check John over, I feel a tear running down my cheek, but not a sad tear!

John is swiftly given the all clear and is guided off to somewhere else in this magnificent building, to start his new life. Annie approaches me, to congratulate me once more, on a great job well done. "You should be proud of yourself Greg", she says. "That was a very important moment in the history of Tx3 and the World! Once John has settled in and is ready, we have the most exciting project I was telling you about, that we want him to drive forwards. There is a great threat coming our way in the near future and we believe John has the capabilities and ideas to solve this great threat, before it happens. If he is successful, the World will never even realise there was a threat in the first place, let alone hear of the great difference that John made. I am very confident, but I guess time will tell, "Annie then suggests I head home, "tell your wife you finished early to help with the cooking and getting the children ready for whatever club they have tonight". Annie smiles at me, as she starts to walk away... "you never know, you might even get back into her good books"? Annie has done it yet again, always a few steps ahead of me and always knowing what is happening.

Thirteen

I arrive home in the middle of the afternoon and feel like I am doing something naughty. I am getting paid for a job that doesn't feel like work and even when I do go into work I sneak off early. This is certainly a dream scenario and life is starting to feel good and balanced again.

The house is quiet and empty, it's like the calm before the storm. The twins will be rushing through the front door any time soon, type of storm. I have just enough time to get the food on the go, when the quietness disappears in an instant. They burst in through the front door, with Bonnie herding them like mad sheep. I try to be as positive as I can, shouting, "hello", to them all, as the twins run straight at me. "How are you home already", they are shouting, as they hit me around my waist. "I have a really nice new boss", I tell them, "one that lets me leave work early so I can cook your food, before you head back out again". They are clearly happy to see me, which is more than I can say for Bonnie. I try and keep the chat going, "I thought it would be nice for us to have food together and I can then take them to their swimming lessons". Bonnie gives me a very forced smile and says to the twins (not to me), "that will be nice don't you think"? This is pretty much how the rest of the time goes, before we head off out once again.

When we arrive back home, Bonnie takes control of getting the twins into their beds and then disappears off for a shower and bed herself. I am left downstairs alone again, in the emptiness with another cold beer. It doesn't seem to taste the same when I am sat here worrying about my relationship and the issues we are clearly having. I always try my hardest to be a good husband and father and most of the time I seem to get things wrong. Yet again I've made things worse when all I am trying to do is make it right. I realise I still haven't told Bonnie how much money I am earning in this new job, or how much money I have in my bank from the golden handshake. It's not like I'm trying to hide it or anything, but between the twins, their clubs and work we haven't been alone long enough to discuss it. Then of course, there was the disagreement this morning which didn't exactly help! The longer this goes on though, the more difficult it will become and the more Bonnie will be convinced it is all a big conspiracy for me to hide things from her. Yet again I have somehow managed to make a really good situation, into a really difficult situation. I'm going to go upstairs right now and break the ice with Bonnie. I can explain how I am trying to do the right thing, how I believe Bonnie needs a break and I can throw in the money situation, as a reason why the holiday can happen.

As I reach the bedroom Bonnie has already turned the light out and is facing away from my side of the bed, as a clear sign of leave me alone. This in fairness is not a new thing, regardless of our argument this morning. I can't remember the last time Bonnie made any attempt to cuddle with me, which hurts. I decide to try and cuddle her and to start a conversation, but Bonnie immediately tells me to go to sleep and to leave her alone as she is very tired. This is just today's excuse as Bonnie probably believes I am going to try it on with her, as men do, to try and make things right, when in fact it just makes things worse. This is clearly not my intention but if I continue, Bonnie will be in a bad mood for many more days. So as usual, I just turn over to face the other way, to be alone in my own thoughts once again.

As I lie here, thinking about today and John's arrival, I feel all warm inside. I'm just starting to relax in my memories, when I suddenly remember what Christian said about my next job. He said they already have another John lined up and how it will be more difficult next time, which clicks my brain right back into gear, with lots of questions whirring around. Who is this John? where will my job take me this time? or more importantly what year will this job take me to? This is a very surreal experience and not one I need going around my brain, as I try to get off to sleep. I then try to kid myself into thinking I can take the rest of the week off work. I can drive around in my beautiful car, visit a coffee shop or two and enjoy not being in there for work reasons. Although I already know deep down, that I will be going into work tomorrow. The temptation of a new project is just too much for me.

Fourteen

The alarm clock ringing out, as if enjoying the fact it has ruined my deep sleep, is how my day starts. I turn over wondering why Bonnie hasn't switched it off, Bonnie however isn't in bed, or even in the bedroom and as I discover, she isn't even in the house. I find a lovely note to the twins, saying she needed to go into work early and she will see them later at school pick-up. I am clearly still in the dog house for having the audacity to suggest we take a holiday.

Having sorted the twins out for school, I leave them with their friends and teachers and I'm free to start my day. I sit in my car, with the radio playing and take deep breaths. I am actually enjoying this new way of starting the day. No arguments at home, no early phone calls from work, no rushing straight from the school to a meeting. It is just a calm, stress free start to the day and I like it. My drive to Tx3 can only be described as wonderful. Sun glasses on, all the traffic appears to be moving in my direction and even when the lights are on red, they are not on red for long. Occasionally I catch sight of a few stressed out people in their cars, or people driving past me fast, only for me to catch them up at the next set of traffic lights. I am not just driving to work, but it's like I'm out for a Sunday afternoon drive.

I soon arrive at the electric gates, which are yet again wide open, welcoming me in. Considering the type of work being done here and the amount of equipment, you'd think the security would be better. Leaving the gates open all the time, is surely wrong. As I enter the building, my keys already handed over, I stand to admire the racing car, the openness of the building and the surroundings in general. A voice suddenly breaks the silence and as I turn, Christian is standing there staring at me. "What on earth are you doing", he asks. "Have you forgotten your way to your office already"? Feeling a little awkward, "I am taking the time to enjoy my life a little more and not rush from one place to another". Christian still staring at me, says,"Time eh, if I'm being honest with you, I've forgotten what rushing from one meeting to another was like. I've been doing this job for several years now and when I left my old IT job, I was just like you. It's as if the World suddenly spins a little slower, it's as if there are suddenly more hours in a day and the green grass looks greener. It annoyed my wife at the time", Christian recalled, "she's a nurse you see and a bloody good one at that. She rushes around all day saving people's lives, which is a good thing. I on the other hand, no longer get stressed and no longer rush around and this drives her mad, as I'm too relaxed. I feel much healthier for it physically and mentally as well. This is no longer a job for me, it's somewhere I come for a few hours, everyday and I absolutely love it". I can't agree more and not only does Christian make me feel part of the team by sharing a bit of his personal life, but he also makes me feel normal. Beyond Christian's external bravado, there is a genuine, caring and decent man on the inside.

We both head off to the inner parts of the building and into Christian's main domain. "Do you know how John is doing this morning"? I enquire. Christian confirms, "he is doing just great. You'll be able to visit him in a day or so as he would have acclimatised fully by them. Apparently he had a good sleep, ate a decent breakfast and is about to start his training for the day. Nothing too heavy I'm told, just a little swim and an introduction into the project they have earmarked for him. Once he's seen a glimpse of the project, I'm sure his brain will start firing up with ideas of where he can help. Now, I know you're interested in John, but I bet you're itching to find out about your next John"?

"Absolutely right I am", is my instant reply, without any hesitation. "Okay, we will go through the process, just like we did with your first John to make sure you are ready and then send you off to do your magic. What I can tell you right now though, is your next John is the one and only John Lennon"! I shakily reply, "THE John Lennon!! The one and only legend Beatle"? "Yep that's the one", is the cheeky sounding reply from Christian. "But how the friggin hell am I supposed to get close to him, let alone talk to him".

"Aha", smirked Christian, with his usual, I am brilliant, look on his face, that I am starting to get used to. "Let me give you some evidence or confidence if you like, that this can work. There are many well known and brilliant people that we have successfully transported here. A perfect example of this would be the King. That was no easy case and it took several trips but we got there in the end and that's all that matters". I realise I am standing with my mouth wide open, before stumbling out my question, "What King"? Christian knows exactly what he is doing and he enjoys being the centre of attention. "The answer to your question", came his response, "is not what King, he is THE King ... the King of rock and roll, Mr Elvis Presley". Christian delivers his line like a cocky, confident school child, doing the drop mic thing and he is loving it.

"Elvis... Elvis from Graceland Elvis"? My head is swirling with confusion and so I challenge Christian, "how is this evidence, or how is this meant to give me confidence"? "Well this wasn't an easy case at all", he starts, "on paper this looked like an open and shut case. After all if you look at his life from the perspective of history, you'd say he was so deep into drugs that he would sign up straight away. When we first met him, we were able to sow the seeds in preparation, then revisit a few years later and eventually build up to the right time to discuss Tx3 with him".

"The plan is pretty similar for your John, which should give you confidence that we've done this before, so in theory we know what we are doing. The Elvis case was indeed a difficult case though. The initial meetings went fairly well, however what we didn't anticipate, was Elvis being ready for us. So when Rob, the person assigned to the Elvis case, returned to discuss everything with him again, Elvis also had a plan ready in his mind, which threw this case wide open. Elvis was simply magnificent in his wishes, or negotiations for want of a better word. He was very clear that he'd had enough of his lifestyle, but not his life! That is such a hugely significant point. He wanted to stay alive, but to live his life freely and not in a fish bowl. So the only way we could get this to work was to fake his death and leave him to live out his days in peace with his family. This was not only difficult, but it would prove incredibly expensive. Those initial rehab costs, which had to be carried out in complete secrecy and then the costs of keeping him in his lavish world".

"Luckily the plan was carried out very well and the costs were covered by his estate, as he ended up selling millions more records, following his alleged death. The plan and delivery was perfect, well nearly perfect, until one day we saw a photo of him in the papers and the boss at the time was furious apparently. Elvis turned out to be an absolute nightmare in terms of keeping him out of sight. He'd spent so many years in the limelight, that it was incredibly difficult for him to no longer have the attention he craved. So from time to time he would be spotted and we would have to deny it was him. The job was made a whole lot easier of course, with the many nut jobs out there, who pretend to be him. However the company's patience was tested to the extreme when he was photographed on his 82nd birthday, at Graceland. He was convinced that as he had died several years before, no one would recognise him, after all he was a much older man, sporting a big white beard. The problem is that a picture like this would get the photographer a massive pay cheque. So when they looked at the photos they had taken that day, they suddenly realised there is this man, that strangely resembles a dead Elvis and Boom, the World goes mad. As you can imagine that was one hell of a mess to clean up".

"We went with the standard line of conspiracy theories and it eventually calmed down, but what we can't control, is the internet. If you searched Elvis Presley conspiracies, even today, you will see the story and more annoying, the photo of him stood right there. This was the last straw, the bosses had accepted the odd photo popping up of him now and then, they went ballistic when he appeared in the film "Home Alone", Elvis was so blatant about it as well, but this photo on his birthday was the final straw".

"The final order was given, that if he was ever spotted again, the contract would be terminated. That was a really difficult meeting for Rob to manage. Ultimately a trust had been built up over several years, which certainly paved the way for the right result, but it shows that relationship are everything in this game. We had given Elvis and his family a golden ticket to enjoy a new found freedom and this had gone on a lot longer than anyone had anticipated. We knew he didn't die from a heart attack in 1977, as Rob had made sure that was brilliantly staged, on that alleged, fateful August. But forty odd years of looking after him, was a huge surprise to us all. However the day eventually came, when we could welcome him here and surprisingly that was just over a year ago. Elvis arrived and settled into his new life very quickly. He has already helped several other singers, with some issues they've been having", Christian tapped his nose and smiled. "He has already proved to be invaluable to the next generation and there was no way we could just let him go, he has even put on a show or two for us, which is just amazing".

"You will get to meet him I'm sure, but you need to be aware he now goes by the name of Aron, with one A at the beginning, not two, he was insistent on that for some reason? Anyway I would be lying if I said I was best mates with Aron, as Rob certainly holds that title. What I can say, having met him several times, he is annoyingly funny, entertaining and a thoroughly lovely man - everything you would wish him to be".

"So what I'm trying to say is, we have the best team, the best support and the best set up here. So we are confident that we can put you in the best possible position to meet and befriend John Lennon. You will have your work cut out, but anything is possible. After all, nothing can be more difficult than the Elvis, or I should say, the Aron case. That took us 8 working days of our time and several months of actual placement time for Rob to complete, with visits over several different years. The payback though, well that's priceless".

Christian led me through to his den, his place of work, with computers, lights and switches everywhere. I have only been in this room a few times, but every time I have been impressed by the sheer amount of technology. As we sit down, Christian tells me of the plan Tx3 have been working on. "We have been able to pin point the various locations that match the times and dates of where John Lennon has been. You can meet up with him several years before he finds fame and fortune. The earliest and most realistic date for you to start this process is back in the summer of 1957, when John was a teenager. Any earlier and it will just be too creepy for a man of your age, to be hanging around with him".

Annie and two other ladies walk in on our meeting, chatting with each other. "Good morning Greg", one of them says, "we are here to put you through your paces and get you ready for your trip. I'm Doctor Douglas and I'm very pleased to be meeting you at last, I've also heard all about your last success, congratulations". I smile, feeling slightly awkward at being congratulated as I've not really been praised during my lifetime. I'm the sort of person that brushes any praise to one side, usually commenting on it being nothing at all, or I generally just put myself down. A good friend of mine, once told me not to do it, as it devalues what I have done. There's no need to start gloating, but a simple thank you is the perfect response. So in response to Doctor Douglas' praise, I simply smile and reply, "thank you" and it did indeed feel like the right thing to do.

Doctor Douglas introduces me to her colleague, Ms D Rees, which sounds very important and intriguing. Ms Rees half smiles, nodding a sort of hello but doesn't elaborate on her job role or why she is here. Ms Rees is clearly confident enough not to force herself into the conversation and has an aura around her. Doctor Douglas eventually turns to look at Christian, "so you've obviously met this idiot then, no introduction is needed". Finally, she gestures towards Annie and states in a very matter of a fact tone, "of course you already know the big bad boss". It is clearly an inside joke, but I don't feel I can laugh, as I hardly know Annie and she is of course the reason I am here and being paid handsomely for my time as well.

"Right, let's crack on then shall we everyone", comes Annie's authoritative words. "Lets pull up a chair and start throwing some ideas around. We need to know everything you have on our Mr Lennon, what the challenges are, as I'm sure there will be many and ideally some quick wins please. I have a meeting in an hour and a half and it would be good to at least road map the basic ideas of this project. We can all then head home, to get a good night sleep, before working on the finer details tomorrow".

Fifteen

We finish with a clear road map apparently, of the job in hand. I don't really know what the plan is, as the team were jumping around with dates, venues and so many names. I decided after about twenty minutes to just nod occasionally and look interested, when in reality I hope I will get a full debrief when the plan is finalised.

At one point in the meeting, Ms Rees said something about the swinging sixties, the sexy fashions, wine and women and from that part onwards I was formulating my own plan. Not a work plan, but a plan of how I can buy Bonnie some expensive lingerie and wine and seduce her. The plan went from zero to one hundred miles an hour in thirty seconds flat. The meeting soon finishes and I am now heading excitedly towards my car. I am walking as quickly as I can without appearing to be rushing out the building like a child leaving school for summer break. I have a naughty glint in my eye and a cheeky grin on my face as I say goodbye to several people on the way.

My car is yet again parked outside, waiting for me, like it is a perfect servant forever on call. Always clean, tidy and just sat here waiting to be started, so I can show off its pleasurable roar. As I drive down the long driveway, I know exactly where I am heading. A little boutique store, a few miles from my house called Millie's, which I have never been into before, as the prices in the window are out of my league. Surely Bonnie will appreciate the effort I'm making and the fact I haven't bought some cheap, slutty tat, but a beautiful and elegant garment. Yes, this present is as much for me as it is for her, but I am a male with needs after all.

I arrive and able to park easily, before strutting confidently into the boutique. The door opens softly and as elegantly as the products they have for sale on the other side. Suddenly I stop in the doorway entrance, as the sheer amount of items for sale hit me. I can feel all of my confidence draining out of me, as if it were seeping down my legs and out of my toes. My legs suddenly feel heavy, unable to move, but light and wobbly at the same time and I am struggling to stay upright. This is a very strange sensation. I must look like a lost school boy, stood in the doorway and certainly not the confident school boy that skipped out of work earlier. Clearly this is noticed by the assistant in the shop, as she ambles towards me, smiling and practically man handling me into the den of iniquity . We have a brief and awkward conversation about why I am here, what I am hoping to achieve with my purchase and eventually they type of look I am going for. The assistant makes the whole process of purchasing sexy items, feel like I am simply buying some fruit and veg, she is incredibly good at her job. I am able to relax a little and by the time I have finished spending just over three hundred pounds, I have even more confidence that the little sexy black item, I am purchasing will have Bonnie wanting me tonight. The assistant wraps the items in some pointless, pretty paper, ties the paper with a bow and sprays them with some perfume, before eventually putting them into a bag which has Millie's, emblazoned on it. I am just standing here waiting, while all this is done, practically urging her to hurry up, as I just want to get out of the shop before anyone else enters. I know women love all the fancy wrapping but I really don't see the point. I'm confident

Bonnie will simply rip open the gift and put the paper and bow straight in the bin.

Smiling awkwardly, as I take the bag to leave, the shop assistant, prolongs the awkwardness, "I hope you get the evening you want. As a tip though, please don't just walk through your front door and give her the present. You need to set the scene, invite her for food and drinks, make it a date night. Tell her to go and buy something new to wear for your date night and you will pay for it, then give her the gift when she returns from her shopping trip". I must look like an alien from another planet, this is clearly great advice and with her being a lady, she will know what Bonnie wants. I on the other hand am thinking of doing the complete opposite and just plan on giving Bonnie the present tonight.

As I drive home though, I play that last conversation over and over in my mind, surely I know my wife better than some shop assistant who has never even met her. However, deep down I know I have to follow her advice, women just know about these things. So as I arrive home, I leave the present in the boot of the car, so I can sneak it into the house another day, when Bonnie is at work.

The usual chaos engulfs me as I open the front door, like a flamed backdraft hitting me in the face. The kids are on top form, telling me about their day at school. Bonnie is stood at the cooker, her back facing me, stirring a pot and looking incredible. I take a moment to ask myself if she looks beautiful because I have been shopping for a fancy outfit, or if I have recently stopped paying her attention, because of all the arguments. I am fully aware that I find a person more attractive, when they are nice to me. If there are ongoing arguments, or low moods, then I simply switch off and cannot cope with the situation, which a psychologist would pin to a point in my childhood no doubt. I move towards Bonnie, with the hope of starting the evening off in a good mood, put my arms around her waist, kiss her cheek, asking, "how was your day"? Bonnie doesn't really move much, other than to continue stirring the food. She does however say, very quietly, "my day was horrible. I know I have been horrible to live with recently and I know what the reason is, my job is sucking the life out of me and I am not sure how much longer I can go on". I turn Bonnie around and cuddle her, before standing back slightly showing her the biggest smile I can muster up, "Bonnie, that's great news". Bonnie's face is already turning to a scrunched up look, as if I haven't been listening to anything she has just said. "How is that great news"? Bonnie angrily snaps. I smile back at her, "I have some great news about my new job, now before you say anything about me not listening, the great news is, you can give up your job if you want to and we can really start living again. You can go and work for a charity if you want to, you can do whatever you want to do, but you no longer need to do the things you don't want to do. Look, as ever we have the twins to sort out and I need to take them to football tonight, but we really need to talk. You told me recently that I hated my job and I am looking for a way to escape, or however you worded it, but it is not the case. I really like my new job and I have just discovered I receive a lot of benefits with it, which we need to talk about. When I am out with the twins tonight, please can you find a babysitter for tomorrow night, I will book a table somewhere and we can go out, like we used to. I can tell you all about my job and how I believe it will change our lives. You can tell me all about your job and the problems you're having and we can start making some decisions about where our lives go from here. What do you think"? Bonnie's face changes to a face I don't think I have ever seen before, let alone can read. Bonnie cautiously replies with a, "yes, okay then, but let's not go to a really posh place, as I don't have anything decent to wear, as I am not as slim as I used to be". I give her another hug, "you'd look amazing to me, even if you were wearing a plastic bag". I then remembered the shop assistants advice, so suggest, "why don't you phone in sick for work tomorrow and instead go and spend the day shopping for something to wear on our date night? Just put it on the credit card and I will take care of the cost, don't skimp and enjoy having some "me" time, as you deserve it. I will pick the kids up from school so you don't need to rush back for them and we can go and have a night on the tiles". Bonnie clearly isn't sure we can afford all of this, but agrees to the plan.

As I stand watching the kids play football, I contemplate the turn of events this evening. Things have gone a lot better than planned and following the shop assistants advice, has more than paid off. The part I am especially proud of, is finally getting to the stage where I can tell Bonnie about the money in my bank account, the wage I am receiving and hopefully I can help to resolve her work issues. Surely by the end of tomorrow night, our lives will be back on track.

Sixteen

The next morning I awake to the usual alarm and the house is alive to the usual complaints about breakfast, the school uniform and bags not packed. This time however, the stress seems subdued and Bonnie is humming tunes, happily getting herself and the twins ready. The atmosphere is completely different to what I'd experienced recently. As I leave for work, Bonnie even gives me a kiss, not a standard because she feels she has to kiss, but a genuine, I might like you again kiss. This means, as I start my drive to work, life feels good, the music is loud, pumping out a hit from the 80's, with my sunglasses on and a smug grin on my face. I am even able to book the restaurant for tonight while driving to work, today is going to be a good day.

Arriving at work, is still such an experience, as I head up the long, sweeping driveway to the magnificent entrance. After handing over my keys, I make my way to my office. Christian has already left me a note, asking me to find him, when and as he put it, if I can be bothered to turn up to work today.

As I enter Christian's domain, I can hear him chatting on the phone, I knock loudly so he knows I am here. Christian gestures me in and he tells the person that he needs to go, as he is just going into an important meeting. Which as he tells me, once he hangs up the phone, "is clearly not true as it is only you I want to speak with". Christian takes me over to his PC and explains how they have now completed the planning stages. He brings up the draft schedule on the screen, showing me that very soon, they will be ready for me to set off to find my new target. That sounds exciting but, "I'm still not completely sure of the plan". Christian laughs, pointing out, "you don't need to know everything", he continues, "just like your last job, you will be given everything you need along the way. In reality you just need to figure it out as you go and we will almost certainly be directed by you". This is music to my ears, Christian also winks, "when you arrive a very familiar agent will be there to meet with you. We just want you to make a very short trip to meet and engage with John very briefly". Christian slowly repeats the phrase, "very briefly" like I am some kind of idiot that can't follow instructions. I look at him like I have lasers beaming out of my eyes at him, "I know what very briefly means". Christian then continues, "the reason it's important for the contact to be brief, is for you to look slightly familiar and friendly to him, when you meet the following time. We know from years of research that this works, so please just follow the instructions". I know Christian is treating me like a two year old, as he continues, "we know exactly where he will be and when, we just need you to be there, simple eh. The next time you go, you will have more to do, but as ever, let's worry about that next time".

I am happy with the plan, I'm raring to go and the sooner the better, as I need to be back in time to pick the kids up from school, which I also point out to Christian in the hope he will hurry things up. In fairness to Christian, he clicks his fingers and points toward me smiling, then says, "don't worry I've got your back. I will get it all set up now, so you can be there and back in plenty of time to get changed and head off to collect the kids from school". Christian maybe a right character, as my parents would say, but in fairness he is also a nice guy.

"Just remember, as it stands we have lost him forever, but if we can get him to sign up to the project, we secure his future immediately. We can get him back here to Tx3 and boom, a huge part of our culture has been saved forever. Imagine, no pun intended, what he can achieve after 1980, the music industry will be better off for it and we as a company get to earn millions in royalties for the work we sell! Genius or what? Those millions then get fed straight back into this project, so we can save more people, politicians, scientists, the list is endless. We just need to save John, then who knows who Annie has lined up for us next"?

It feels pretty exciting, it's suddenly very real and I genuinely feel like I am changing the World and the course of history. I also feel eager to get started, so I can get back home in time for the twins and course my date night with Bonnie.

Following a short debrief to confirm I am heading to Liverpool in June 1957, I change into my 1950's clothes, the ones I'd used last time. It is like meeting an old friend and all the memories come flooding right back. In fact, I am actually going to meet an old friend, Tom, who apparently will travel from the USA, on a so called business trip to meet me in Liverpool. Today we will enjoy a cup of tea in a cafe, briefly meet John, but not engage too much. This is the perfect set up for the meetings to come, apparently.

I head to the most exciting room in the building, step onto the now familiar round, slightly raised platform and just like last time I nod to Christian, to confirm I am ready. The machine whirs, blue lights flash and my excitement levels rise even more than last time. The reality is I am not scared this time, as I now know what to expect. Then, just as before I am in the 1950's, but this time in a house, in Liverpool. This will never get boring, what an epic buzz, time travelling is.

I quickly scan the room and see the usual folder containing the details that I will need, including where to meet Tom and what time. I have twenty minutes to wait and a five minute stroll to the cafe. I read about the local area and what is happening at this time, to get me right up to speed. Then before I know it, it is time to leave, time to go and meet the legend that is John Lennon.

"Roses Rooms" is at the end of the street, it is simply incredible and has a fantastic atmosphere, from the moment I open the door. Behind the counter a lady is making tea, who has a sort of mothering look about her. She instantly reminds me of an auntie I once had, who always wore a red and white, or a blue and white, checked apron. She was always immaculate and wanting to give out hugs, it was like she had an internal people magnet, which sucked you right into her hugging arms. I guess the lady is the owner Rose and standing beside her is a happy looking chap, with birds tattooed on his arms, like an old sailor with greased back hair, perfect for this time. The chap smiles a jolly welcome and asks, "what would you like today"? I notice Tom hasn't arrived yet, so order two cups of tea, to which the man states, "you're new around here aren't you". Very observant, but I guess everyone knows everyone around here. With a smile back, I reply, "I'm visiting a friend", then "Viv", came his response... "I'm Viv and this is Rose, as in Roses Rooms. If you need anything just let us know, we have the best breakfast is England and we are always happy to help". What a pleasant place Liverpool in 1957 appears to be. Maybe I can include it on my time travellers holiday destination list, to go with the U.S.A. of course.

I am able to find a little table, right in front of the window, so I can take in the street scene. I can now watch the World go by, British 1950's style. It's like being on a film set, everything is just perfect. People strolling around in their summer clothes looking incredible, except for one man who walks passed, bizarrely in a rain coat and hat, completely covering himself, which I have a chuckle at. Tom enters the cafe, without me noticing, as I'm fascinated with this oddly dressed man. Tom approaches from behind me and slaps both hands onto my shoulders, in a deliberate attempt to startle me, which, in fairness works. I immediately jump up to greet him with a good solid handshake and a slap on his arm. "How are you doing"? I ask, "You look a little younger than the last time I saw you", I suggest, while winking at him. "Yep, it feels weird to meet you again, two years before I met you last time, now that's enough to give someone a headache". We both chuckle at this mind blowing fact, as we sit down. Maybe this is why I had felt a connection to Tom when I last met him?

Following a bizarre exchange of pleasantries Tom is quick to explain the plan. "John will becoming in here shortly, he will sit in the chair just behind us. I'm sure he will want to sit in this chair though, as he likes to look out the window when he's here. That's ok though, as I guess he will be looking over at us, in the hope we move, which of course we won't. We need you to somehow get talking to him briefly, maybe about music, but without it being too obvious. Then we can leave, it's as simple as that. Of course the next time you meet him, you can recall today and the plan slowly fits into place. You all set"?

I am as ready for this as I will ever be, after all it's not every day you meet a Beatle is it. We carry on chatting about Tx3 and how long I've been back, before today's meeting, when out of the corner of my eye I spot him. John casually walks in, orders a pot of tea and appears to know Rose and Viv very well. John turns to take his seat at the window and seems thrown for a second, at the fact we have usurped his plan. Then exactly as Tom said, he takes a seat right behind us. I suddenly feel excited, like it's game on, or better still like I am just walking onto the stage to perform.

We continue to make quiet conversation, making sure to avoid all chat about Tx3. I eventually stand up to get another two cups of tea and make sure to bump into John's table, spilling his tea. "Oh I'm terribly sorry", I immediately say, "let me get you another". In fairness to John, although he is clearly not impressed with my clumsiness, he squeezes out a small smile and accepts my offer. "You can't waste a drop of tea now, can you?", I say to him as I walk up to Rose for our refills and for another pot of John's tea. As I return to John's table I apologise again, but am pleasantly surprised by John's response. "Can't waste a drop of tea eh, I always say this", John says. "Tea is such a wonderful invention and one of the things I must have every single day". My response, isn't the best, but is a simple, "I couldn't agree with you more", followed quickly with, "tea and music make the World go around". John's face lights up, "music yeah, now that's my World".

As tempted as I am to keep the conversation going, I can hear Christians voice, reminding me that I am under strict instructions to make the contact brief. So I just smile back at John and say "it was nice to meet you and sorry again about the tea". I turn and head back to my seat. Tom is grinning from ear to ear and quietly acknowledges, "well I think that all went to plan, everyone will be pleased".

We finish our drinks and as we head towards the door, I nod in John's direction. Viv spots us leaving and shouts a very friendly, "hope to see you in here again soon". As we step out onto the street, the weather is unusually hot and the sun is blinding me. Tom already has his sun glasses on, looking the all American man that he is.

I am relieved the meet went to plan and my work is now finished. Tom suggests we go and celebrate the night away, "after all we can stay for a few days and still get you back home on time". "Let's go to a few pubs and see where the night takes us"? I feel like a right bore and don't really have an excuse not to go, but all I want to do is to get back home. To a date night with my wife, which we hardly ever have, to chat the night away about my job, money, holidays and of course the cheeky black satin outfit I purchased. I am aware I'm drifting off to a much more pleasant time, which is no reflection on Tom's company. I apologise and explain I have a date night set up and waiting for me back home, so I will have to pass on this occasion. Tom smiles a knowing, almost evil smile, "oh that's nice, I'm pleased for you". Then his face turns to a full on devious look, as he says, "well I am going to use my American accent to its full potential here in England". Although he actually pronounces it as, "In,Ger,Land", which always makes me chuckle. English women, according to Tom, "go wild for it, the stories of who I am get more extreme each time. Tonight, I plan on being a surgeon, who has flown in from the states to operate on a child that needed a life saving operation. I am at the top of my field and the only one that can perform this type of surgery in the World. I have just spent six hours in the operating room, successfully saving the child's life, of course and I am now out having a few drinks to unwind. I only have this one night, here in beautiful Liverpool, before I need to head back to my Malibu pad. Trust me, I plan on having the time of my life. Are you really sure you won't come with me? We could be the only two surgeons in the World that can perform this incredibly delicate operation... come on, this could be a free night, a holiday for a job very well done today AND of course you will still be back home at the same time. It doesn't matter if you stay with me for a few hours or a few days God damn it, the result is still the same. Hey, you can even get some practice in before your hot date tonight". Tom is smiling from ear to ear, winking at me and pulling my arm in the opposite direction to the house that I came from earlier.

"Okay, okay Tom", I hear myself saying, "just a few drinks though. I'm happy to play along with your sordid story, but I won't be a fellow doctor, I will be your driver. That feels less complicated and".... I'm interrupted by Tom saying, "please don't call me Tom, my name is now Doctor Tom", he then bursts out laughing. I shake my head and make it clear, I am going with him under duress, but in reality I am quite looking forward to having a boys night out. It's not often I get to go out on the town these days, as I've usually been working, or running around with the twins. I am happy to have a few drinks, relax and catch up properly with

Tom, maybe get a bite to eat and then head off to bed for a lovely, uninterrupted night of sleep. Hell, I can even stay in bed and have a lazy morning, without the school run. Then once I have fully recovered, I can head back home ready for my date night. Perfect ! A mini break is just what the doctor ordered, well, Doctor Tom that is!

We enter a pub about ten minutes later, following a gentle stroll in this glorious weather. We find a booth, with two benches and a table in between us. Tom order the beers and brings them over to me, with a huge smile on his face. "Don't tell me", I say, "you've pulled already haven't you". Tom places the beers down onto the table and still smiling, says, "nope I haven't, but that was the cheapest round of beers I've bought in a long time. This pub has certainly captured my heart". As we sit talking about life and the weird twists and turns it takes you on, Tom is constantly looking around the room for some female company.

Tom suddenly spies a very pretty blonde lady, sitting alone at a table, wearing a military uniform. I don't know what type of military uniform it is, but I can see it fits her perfectly. As much as I try not to be a typical man, ogling at her, I can't help but agree with Tom that this lady is indeed beautiful. She is easily the prettiest lady in the place and the prettiest lady I've seen in an awfully long time. Tom is over the moon and is itching to go and speak to her, but I can tell he feels tied to me, as he dragged me out in the first place. After watching Tom squirm for a few minutes, I eventually say, "you should go and speak with her and see how it goes". I'm expecting Tom to say no, in the first instance at least, but I am wrong. Tom shoots off like he has a lit firework up his backside. I continue to sit here drinking my beer and glancing over at the two of them talking. I watch the locals come and go and the room is filled with the sounds of a piano, being played by an old man in the corner. Occasionally he sings along, when he can remember the odd word or two. The air is filled with smoke as pretty much everyone in the pub appears to be smoking cigarettes or pipes. I'm trying to remember the last time I've sat down, by myself, with a pint of beer, as I'm usually running around with the twins. Tom on the other hand, continues to chat to the lady and he is getting louder by the minute, as his inner show off American self, kicks in. He is clearly loving being the centre of attention and tells his usual jokes to a whole new captured audience. I wonder if I could live here for a few years, no stress, clearly no financial worries and when I get bored I could just pack up and go back to my date night with Bonnie. I would buy a beautiful house, a car and even marry the military lady and when she gets bored of me, I can return home.

After an hour of sitting alone, I decide there is only so much time I can spend sitting here doing nothing. I stand, waving at Tom to let him know I am going to leave him to it. I decide to wave and leave all at the same time, as I don't want Tom to rush after me, in an attempt to convince me to stay. Yet again and to my further surprise, Tom just waves back and instantly turns back to carry on their chat.

I walk quickly out of the door and onto the street. I'm headed straight back to the house, as I am ready to get comfy and sleep for hours in a deep peaceful sleep. My brain on the other hand has different ideas and reminds me of my date night. I try to ignore the thoughts and I try to convince myself that sleep is much more important right now. However, the house is cold and unwelcoming and I immediately reach a decision, that I'm going to head home. I even ask myself if I will have any regrets about leaving, then chuckle about talking to myself, but deep down I know I am ready. Before I can talk myself out of it, I initiate the boomerang to leave.

Seventeen

I am immediately back at Tx3, with Christian
staring at me, leaning against a machine with his
arms folded. "What took you so long", comes his
rhetorical question. "Some of us have work to do",
is all I can muster up as a reply, "anyway I wasn't
gone that long, was I". "Long enough for me to
walk a few steps and lean on here to wait, anyway,
lets get the debrief done, then I guess you will be
wanting to head off for the school run, as you're
very nearly working enough hours to be classed as
a part-timer, these days", Christian says, in a very
sarcastic tone.

The debrief is indeed short, as I explain how I met John, how it unfolded and how I left him at Roses Rooms. Strangely enough I decide not to mention the trip to the pub with Tom as I don't really think it is relevant. I do however confirm it went according to plan, but I'm not overly eager to keep the conversation going. Christian is satisfied with the outcome and cheekily states, "well you are free to leave", like he's my boss. After I have a quick shower and change I am out of here, heading to the car and the school run and eventually home to get ready for my date night. Just as I start the car, I see Christian driving past me, in a loud Mercedes and the cheeky sod is clearly getting off work, just early as me. He even salutes me as he drives past, with a huge grin on his face. I casually pull away behind Christian, he is driving like his life depends on it and is quickly out of sight.

My drive home consists of me drifting off constantly, day dreaming about what might happen tonight. I arrive at the school on time and worryingly, I can't remember half of my trip here. The twins come running to the gates to meet me and we hug like we haven't seen each other for months. It is incredible how I instantly appreciate this little moment in my life and I just know I will remember this simple moment forever. The drive home is full of chatter, both of them talking at the same time, with me just nodding and agreeing, without actually knowing what they are talking about. Then we all burst through the front door, loud and laughing, straight into Bonnie, who is pretty much ready to go and looking a million dollars. Also nan and grandad are here sitting patiently waiting for us to arrive. The twins go berserk as they realise they are having a night away and will no doubt be spoiled rotten. I on the other am also going berserk internally, as I realise we are definitely going to have a full night without the twins, we can make as much noise as we want and we don't have to get up early in the morning.

Bonnie is explaining their bags are all packed, nan and grandad are taking them out for pizza and a sleepover and they will be dropping them to school in the morning. Tick, tick, the list is all being ticked off in my mind and I feel incredibly happy. Bonnie makes sure they know one of us will pick them up after school tomorrow, as I help put their bags in the boot of the car and wave them off. Bonnie heads straight back into the house, so she can finish getting ready. I on the other hand, hang back so I can collect the "Millie's" present from my car and then swagger confidently back into the house. Bonnie is already in the bathroom, doing her finishing touches, as she puts it. "I will be ready in about half an hour", she calls out.

I have never showered, shaved and dressed into a smart suit so quickly in all my life. As I enter the bedroom Bonnie is sat, like a model on the end of our bed. Her new dress has a long split up the side and she is showing me her legs and an incredible pair of high heeled shoes. I can't help but stop in my tracks and all I can say is, "wow you look amazing". Bonnie blushes, but is clearly pleased with my reaction. I hand her the present and Bonnie opens it carefully, making sure not to rip the paper or the bow wrapped around it, then carefully takes out the incredibly skimpy black outfit. Raising an eyebrow at me, she says, "you'll need to be a very lucky man for me to put this on". I feel and probably look like a horny teenager, "I am half wondering if we should scrap the meal and just stay home to play"? In fairness I already know the answer, as Bonnie puts the bag to one side, smiling, "I tell you what, I will put it on for you one night as a surprise". I'll take that and know this is probably code for, I will wear it for you later after a few drinks.

We order a taxi and arrive shortly after, at a very posh and expensive restaurant. It is so posh I can't pronounce the name above the door. We are greeted by a young, very posh sounding gentleman in a penguin suit, who seats us by the window over looking the river. A perfect setting, hopefully for a perfect night ahead of us.

The waiter returns quickly with an open bottle of champagne, as requested by moi, when I booked the table. He pours the golden bubbly liquid into our very expensive looking glasses, which Bonnie finishes in two swigs. "It's nice in here", she says, pouring herself another glass, "are you sure we can afford it though". I feel calm and centred as I confirm, "absolutely, now relax, enjoy the bubbles and our first, adult only night out in a long time". Raising my glass, to a toast, "cheers and here's to a good night ahead". "Cheers", Bonnie says back to me, downing another glass of champers straight away.

"Now, why are we here, what is really happening with your job"? Bonnie blurts out. "How can it possibly change our lives, come on, I need to know everything". I start to explain everything, from my meeting with Annie and how they had watched me for a while and although it sounded big headed, they felt I would be perfect for the job. "What exactly is the job though", asks Bonnie, genuinely interested, which I haven't experienced from her in a long time. "Well, that's a little complicated", as I try to buy myself some time to think about my next response, "the job is pretty much meeting prospective clients, so I can explain the benefits of the company and how we feel our ideas align perfectly with theirs". Bonnie rolls her eyes to the back of her head, then pours herself another glass, "okay", she announces, "I wish I'd never asked now. So in short it's a very similar job to the last one you had, but a posher car and bit more money". Bonnie's tone has suddenly changed from an excited, giggly, date night tone, to a disappointed, oh this isn't going to change our lives after all, sounding tone.

I pause for a few seconds watching her, wondering if I am enjoying the anguish and disappointment she is feeling. Or if I am also disappointed that Bonnie feels my job doesn't quite hit her expectations and the night is going to be crap. However, I am also pleasantly pleased that I don't need to go into any more detail. I can quickly gloss over this part and therefore not have to lie about what I actually do. "To answer your question", I retort, "yes it's a similar job, with a posher car, but here's where it gets really interesting", I say. To use a fishing term, Bonnie is now back on the hook, leaning forward in anticipation of my next words. The young waiter reappears right on cue, as if to stop me bursting all the details to Bonnie at once. I almost say, and all will be revealed after the break, but I am too embarrassed, as the waiter is trying to take our order. Ordering food is simple, fish starter for me, soup for Bonnie, followed by steak for me and the vegetarian option for Bonnie. I don't really need to look at the menu and with that the waiter leaves us once again.

Bonnie smiles, then looks around the room, as if to check no one is within ear shot, and then prompts me to continue. "Where was I", I start again, knowing damn well I know exactly where I was. "Oh yes, this is where it gets interesting". I tell Bonnie how I played hard ball with Annie and how, if they really wanted me, they would need to stretch the budget to get me. Bonnie rolls her eyes again, "it's not like you are a professional football player, that's the signing of the century, is it"? "Agreed", I acknowledge, "but based on my knowledge of the sector and the experience I've gained over the years, they don't want me to simply do the same job as before, they want me to practically run the company". Boom, there it is, I lie to Bonnie's face and worryingly I didn't even flinch and even more worryingly I don't feel guilty. Maybe Tom has rubbed off on me after all.

Bonnie just glares at me and I am convinced she is about to tell me I am a liar. Instead she bursts out laughing, but then she strangely starts to cry. I can suddenly sense people in the restaurant, looking at us and whispering. I can imagine them thinking I have just asked for a divorce or something along those lines. Bonnie starts to apologise, "oh I'm so sorry, I bet you think I'm horrible. I didn't ask you about your job interview and more to the point I wasn't even listening when you tried to tell me. I haven't let you share your new job news with me at all and you must have been bursting to share it with me". I just sit there, as I wonder who has stolen my wife. From all the years we've been together, Bonnie has not once apologised and she certainly has never used the word, sorry. At best, if Bonnie realises something is her fault, she will just go into an incredibly happy place to over compensate for the issue, when in all reality a simple, "sorry", will do. Now, in the middle of this restaurant, Bonnie is crying and saying sorry to me. I should be embarrassed, but it actually feels nice to finally hear the word, "sorry", coming out of her mouth. I feel in control, so maybe my training at Tx3 is paying off, after all.

"Look, don't worry about it, you've had a lot going on with your work as well", is the only sensible response I have. Bonnie stops crying, "it's no excuse, but yes, work has been really shit recently". I take a sip of the champagne before asking, "so what's happening at your work then, why is it suddenly all shit there"? Bonnie immediately looks uncomfortable and is quick to try and dismiss the question, but I want to know, as it is clearly upsetting her. Bonnie smiling timidly, "you won't shout will you"? "Now since when have I ever shouted", I answer straight back. I am the sort of person that listens to the issue and tries to put a glass half full spin on it. Bonnie, drinks some more, then blurts out the fact that, "my boss is an arsehole". Well it certainly catches my attention, as Bonnie keeps on rambling, "he's a right pig who treats me like a dumb girl and recently he slapped my arse and made it obvious he wanted me to have sex with me". Now, in fairness, that is not the response I was expecting and I am wondering how I can put a positive spin on that? "Hmm okay, so why didn't you tell me before and what have you done about it".

Bonnie is trying to hold back the tears and keep it together, just as our food arrives, for what feels like another commercial break! Bonnie soon continues, "I just feel so ashamed, like you might think I've done something wrong, or you might think I led him on in some way", which she makes abundantly clear, is not the case, "and no, I haven't done anything about it at all, I haven't even told a work friend". So there it is, as Bonnie puts it, "the explanation of why I've been a right grumpy cow recently". Typically of me, I spout out, without thinking, "but why have you been a right grumpy cow for the past ten years then"? in an attempt to

make light of it. "So what am I going to do"?
Bonnie whispers across the table to me, her eyes
filled with despair in the hope I will have the
solution to her problem.

"Well I do have an idea", I smile warmly back at
her. "Let me be a little selfish and finish telling you
about my job and I think the solution will become
obvious". Bonnie just nods, a confused look on her
face, as she finishes her drink and pushes her
starter away, "I'm not that hungry really". It is now
my turn to roll my eyes playfully at her and I
gesture the waiter over. "Shall we just settle up and
go to the cocktail bar around the corner"?

Eighteen

Five minutes later, the bar around the corner welcomes us in with their music and cocktails and what appears to be nice comfy seats. "What'll you have sir", asks the lady behind the bar? This is always an easy reply for me, when I'm in a cocktail bar. I only know one cocktail and that's a "sex on the beach", cocktail. So I naturally order that, while Bonnie scours the menu and eventually settles for a "cosmopolitan" as it will cheer her up, apparently.

Taking our seats in the corner, with our drinks in hand, it feels appropriate to say "cheers" and for some bizarre reason I add, "bottoms up", just before taking a healthy slurp of my drink. Bonnie however, just sits glaring at me, "was that supposed to be funny? I tell you about my boss slapping my arse and you think it's amusing to say bottoms up." "Ha ha", I slowly agree, "no pun intended, now come on drink up". That was strangely another thing that Bonnie took literally at my word. With another drink gone, I am encouraged to follow suit and she swiftly orders another round. "Soooo", came the slightly slurring question, "soooo, what's happening with your job that'll change our lives"? Bonnie blurts out. I pull my chair in a little closer, Bonnie does the same and I finally get my chance to spill the beans. I start like I am reading a great book. "As I was saying earlier, I have been hired to practically run the company and they wanted to give me a golden handshake for joining, as a way of preventing me

from leaving again, quickly afterwards I suppose".
Bonnie is certainly intrigued, "exactly how much
of a golden handshake are we talking about"?
Bonnie asks, in her best whispering voice, which is
actually louder than her normal talking voice.
"Well this is where the life changer comment
comes from", I grin wildly. I lean in close and
whisper in her ear, "a half a million pound golden
handshake". Then I lean back in my chair, take a
sip of my cocktail and drink in the look on Bonnies
face, as I think to myself, this is a wonderful
moment!

At first Bonnie is quiet and still, just sitting there
smiling, trying to process the information, but then
turns angrily to ask, "why haven't you told me this
before now"? Before I can answer though, Bonnie
changes again to what can only be described as
someone winning the lottery and the emotional
relief that it must bring. Tears, of joy and the
realisation that the stress she has been going

through can be packed up and thrown into the bin, right here, right now. It's an amazing feeling to experience this being played out in front of me. Bonnie downs yet another drink and orders more, again. After a bit of jumping around, she slumps back in the chair exhausted. "So I can give up my job then? I mean I don't need to go back there ever again, right?" "Absolutely", is my proud response, "but only if that's what you really want? Rather than decide tonight, why not take a few days off work and think about it. Oh and by the way, you haven't asked me how much I get paid to do this swanky new job of mine, have you"? Bonnie squints at me to focus, before launching into, "Oh shit, it didn't even cross my mind, are you into six figures"? Smiling I reply, "Nope, not a six figure a year salary". Bonnie sighs, followed by, "well in fairness we don't need a huge salary do we, if we don't have a mortgage, so come on then, hit me with it, how much"? Beaming from ear to ear I whisper, "it's not a six figure salary, it's a seven figure salary". Bonnie is struggling to comprehend my statement and even starts counting noughts on her fingers. "What... are you telling me you are being paid a cool one million pounds a year, on top of the joining amount"? She looks at me with a scrunched face and both hands turned up, like a classic emoji, "Noooo" I smirk, "try four million pounds a year". "Shut up", is all Bonnie can say to me and several times as well. "You are freaking me out now Greg, tell me this is some kind of weird joke, because I don't think I can cope". I guess I've had time for me to digest this information and in fairness I wasn't as drunk as Annie at the time. So I am able to confirm with a dead pan face, "no joke, honestly". Bonnie is fairly quiet for the next few seconds, we are then finally able to have the holiday planning conversation, the nice cars conversation, the twins education and eventually the whole security conversation. We keep drinking and chatting into the small hours of the morning before eventually catching a taxi back home at around three in the morning.

As the taxi drops us back home, I give myself a stern talking to under my breath, "This is it, don't mess this up now", I tell myself. I know I need to play things a bit cool when we get inside the house. Don't rush her up the stairs, send Bonnie on her way, while I get a glass of water and delay for a few minutes. Once we are inside, this works a treat, as I stand in the kitchen, looking around and thinking about how we don't need to move. We have all our memories right here and after tonight, I will have even more memories, in this house. I estimate it will take Bonnie about five minutes to slip into her little black number and after exactly five minutes I start to walk up the stairs. My heart is pumping so hard, I wonder if I might have a heart attack, before I even reach the bedroom. As I approach the bedroom door, I notice the small lamp has been left on, which means I will be able to see

Bonnie in all her glory. Will she be lying on the bed looking seductive, or will she be standing beside it casually, waiting for me? I fling open the door, all manly and Bonnie is lying there in front of me on the bed, but face down, fully clothed and passed out snoring. In fairness, I am often disappointed when going to bed, as I always believe that tonight will be the night, only to discover it isn't tonight yet again. This time though, feels like a knife in the heart and I can practically feel my penis shrinking, like a naughty school boy being told off and my balls feel like they have disappeared, right back up inside me. "Wow", is literally all I can say and not Wow in a good way. I can't even be bothered to undress Bonnie to make her comfy, I just put a blanket over her and sort myself out for bed. As I lie there, starting to drop off to sleep, I recall the highs and lows of the last twenty four hours. From my meeting with John Lennon, through to seeing Bonnie's many faces tonight, as she passed through all her emotions. Now I'm lying in bed listening to Bonnie snoring!

Morning arrives far too quickly, the sun light comes bursting through the curtains, which were only half pulled last night. I drag my hungover body out of bed and make my way downstairs for a drink of water and a slice of toast. As I switch on the TV the breakfast news is being announced, along with the usual depressing stories around the World, while I contemplate how depressing my sex life is. Even when I have all the stars aligned and I am potentially the best husband in the World, I still can't get any. What the hell does a man need to do around here? At least I'm not going into work today and I plan on having a nice long and well deserved, weekend.

Nineteen

Monday morning, a brand new week and I have decided that this will be the beginning of a new me as well. I quite liked the old me, if I'm being honest and I have always been told, you can only ever be yourself, so be the best you, that you can be. The problem is, I'm not getting the best out of me at the moment, I'm too focused on getting my penis some action. Or to put it another way, I'm too distracted on the fact that my penis never gets any action. So I've decided that my life can no longer be ruled by my penis. I am no longer concerned about whether or not I get some action, instead I am going to enjoy every other aspect of my life. I once met a sports player, at a business lunch and he told me that I should always put myself first. He didn't mean I was to be selfish, he explained that if I am fit and healthy and enjoying the things I like in life, then my whole being will be more appealing to others. In turn, others will want to be with me and will be more attracted to me. So my plan, from this day forward, is to get me sorted.

I said my usual goodbyes at home, but made an extra effort with Bonnie. I need to show that I am not being a sulky teenager, because we didn't have any sex over the weekend and I am a happy person. Part of me wonders if Bonnie even realises that we didn't have sex the other night, or does she just assume we did? Either way I'm not going to dwell, "enjoy your day off", I shout, as I find my car keys, to which Bonnie replies laughing, "oh I will, I'm going to spend the day relaxing, no work for me".

As I close the front door, two thoughts instantly cross my mind. The first thought is, good for Bonnie, she doesn't need to go into work and see her idiot boss. The second thought is, I am already exhausted from being this new positive me, it takes so much effort and it's only the first morning, so what chance do I have of keeping this up?

I casually and lethargically stroll into work and worryingly I am no longer blown away by the decor of this amazing building. I force myself to look around and appreciate where I am and to remind myself that the big pay check comes from my being here. So basically, I need to up my game, as many people would literally cut their right arm off to be here. I enter my office, sit down in front of the PC, which I will never need for work. Christian annoyingly pops his head around the door and shouts, "morning dickhead", at me. Not only do I jump, I embarrassingly tell him off, like he is one of the twins. Christian on the other hand just laughs back and says. "Wellllll, you've gotta have a laugh haven't you". Quickly followed by, "so are you ready to tackle the next part of your job? Come on let's get you ready to head off again, you lucky shit".

I follow Christian down a long corridor, like I am following a teacher taking me to the heads office. Annie calls after us, as she is going to join us. "I do like to be here, it's much more exciting than spreadsheets. Besides a few hours or even days away for you, is only a few seconds of my time, which is perfect. Christian has already brought me up to speed, first thing this morning, it's a critical visit this time right? as they all are I suppose". "The plan", as Christian announces to Annie, "is for Greg to meet up with John, but he will be a little older now. John has now met Paul and the band have formed, with his future looking Rosie. They are right at the beginning of their careers and now is the time for Greg to show his face again. Greg you will need to remind John of your first brief meeting, to get his brain whirring". I am certainly ready for this, yes I am a little jaded from the weekend, but I know I am ready.

Annie smiles, "go and get your target and when you get back I need to introduce you to someone called Mark. He may or may not be able to help with this case. Mark is going to be seconded to us from the CIA in a joint project. He is flying in from Beirut where he's been training and the CIA feel he might be able to help us out with this particular job. Anyway, if he's around I will introduce you to him, but I just wanted you to be aware in case you bump into him". I just smile and say, "yeah, happy to meet anyone new, after all I'm still the newbie as well", then I head off to change.

A few minutes later I'm stood in the oh so familiar place. This feels more like my office, than my office does. Christian announces, "all systems are ready, how about you Greg, are you good to go"? I nod, take a deep breath and as I exhale I arrive smoothly in 1960. No exciting countdown from the machine, no tension lights, just a calm transfer. I was informed in the debrief that it will be 27th May 1960 and I will be in Scotland. The band are on tour, as a support act to "Johnny Gentle". I embarrassingly have no idea who Johnny Gentle is and I certainly don't know why they are in Scotland on tour. When I think of the Beatles, I picture them in Liverpool or America with screaming girls everywhere. What I do know, is this is about two and a half years after I had last met John in Roses Rooms. I have no idea if he will remember me, but I will make sure to remind him of that day, which in my World was only last week of course.

I am stood in an old farm house, which is a little cold, damp and clearly from the smell, not used very often. An envelope is on a sideboard waiting for me. This time it is directing me into town, straight down the lane outside this farm house. The town is called "Nairn", a fishing village, with plenty of shops and tonight John will be performing with the band. Interestingly it lists the band as "The Silver Beetles", is this a typo?

I casually meander into town, to have a mooch around in the hopes of bumping into John. I quickly find a quirky cafe and peer through the window, in the hopes of seeing John drinking a cup of tea, but no such luck. Christian did however, make sure he supplied me with a ticket for the concert tonight. As a worst case scenario I can try and see him there, but this is far from ideal. This is going to prove trickier than I'd initially thought. Why hadn't Tx3 told me exactly where John will be, like my last meet? Maybe they simply don't have the data in the systems? After a few hours of generally hanging around, the doors to the hall are opened and I am able to go inside to find a seat.

The room is buzzing with young people and listening to the chatter, it appears they are all here for Johnny Gentle. No one really knows much about this other group, which makes me chuckle. I soon realise I won't be able to get to the front, which makes getting eye contact with John very difficult, so I decide to just see how this plays out, as ever what will be, will be. The Silver Beetles come on stage shortly after and the boys all look incredibly young and handsome. Although they look tired and dare I say it, a little nervous, which surprises me. They start to play and sing and it sounds okay, but not amazing. I remind myself that the technology, speakers, microphones etc are different back in this day and age, but there isn't the same energy that I have seen in the TV clips. The second song is also okay, but I'm not convinced they really know the song, but I guess this is the early Beatles and they are just learning their craft, before the big time will come.

The set comes and goes and I feel a little underwhelmed about my first Beatles, or I should probably say Beetles, concert. Following a short break, Johnny Gentle appears on stage and I know this is my opportunity to get back stage. I push my way past the fans and head for the stage door where I am expecting to meet some security and resistance. As I push open the door I am surprised to find the door unguarded. I carry on down the hallway, until I can eventually hear the boys talking. I knock on the door and stand back, suddenly wondering how I might be received. The one and only Paul McCartney pulls the door open and looks me up and down briefly, before he asks, "what do you want". I can't believe Paul McCartney is standing in front of me, "can I possibly have a quick chat with John"? I ask. Paul glances over his shoulder, as if gesturing to John, who appears around the door. John's greeting, for want of better words, is a tired "sorry pal, what do you want"? Again I smile and take a deep breath, ready to speak, but before I can even say a word, John announces, "hang on! I know you don't I"? I am about to answer, when John pulls me by my shoulder into their room, "come and meet the boys, while I try and figure where I know you from. Don't tell me, it's right on the tip of my tongue". The others are having a few drinks and are looking a bit hot and sweaty. As I sit down in the chair my eyes are drawn towards Paul, who is lifting up a notebook and pen and writing in it. I guess they are lyrics but I don't want to pry, as I don't want to appear nosey. A bottle of beer is suddenly thrust towards me by John, as he pulls up a chair next to me. "So why are you here", John asks,? while clinking the two bottles together? "I wanted to see how you are getting on", is my deliberately vague response. John just laughs, "I like you", he says, "we've definitely met before haven't we"? I laugh along with him and feel strangely comfortable in his company. "Yes we've met before, but I was a bit clumsy the last time, does that help"? John is like a child, all excited at the fact that he knows me, but he can't work out where he knows me from. "Ok, you win" he says, "I just can't think where I know you from". "Well", I say, as if settling in for a story by the fire, "it was a warm summers day, about two and half years ago and we were in the best city in the World". I wink at John and we both say at the same time, "Liverpool". I can see John's brain whirring trying to pull all the details together. "I was sat with a friend enjoying a nice cup of tea and chatting about life, right in the window seat of a great cafe". John is still trying to remember, "well I say cafe, but really I should say Roses Rooms". John's face is a picture as he clearly remembers the place, but not me. "Unfortunately I bumped into your table and spilled some of your tea". John suddenly jumps out of his seat, like he'd been electrified, shouting, "yeah that's it, that's where I know you from". His band members just smile, as they are clearly out of the loop on this one. "Wow yeah, I remember now, man I love that place and I love sitting in the same seat you were in, right in the window, watching the World go by. Damn I knew I recognised you. So what the hell are you doing all the way up here in Scotland"? "I'm actually up here on business, but I am aware you are in this band and you were playing here tonight, so I thought I'd pop in and say hi". "Well I'm pleased you did.. er? Sorry fella, I didn't catch your name before"? "No problem I'm Greg, I'm the man that thinks tea and music make the world go around". "Yeah that's it, that what you said before".

John finishes his drink and slams it on the table, "so come on then Greg, let's go and have a beer across the road and you can tell me what you thought of the gig tonight". The others decline and Paul reminds John, "you need to be on the bus at ten in the morning, so take it easy yeah". These are the last words I hear as the door closes behind us!

We are soon sat in a bar, chatting about life and how things have slowly been working out for John. He tells me that he's had a pretty chaotic upbringing, between his mum, dad and living with his auntie, but he now feels he's found his calling in life, to be playing music to people every night. But with some slight sorrow on his face, he admits, "I'm not where I want to be yet. I want to be writing and playing my own songs, while I'm young. The songs we play right now are covers of other singers, but I want to have our own music out there". He is a vision of a man, as young as he is, he has a certain determination in him that I don't think I've ever seen before and I like that, in fact, I like him.

"So what the hell do you do Greg? I mean it's got to be a pretty strange job, to drag you all the way up here". I hope I look genuine as I reply, "I'm into travel and it literally takes me all over the world, so I can't complain". John loves this, "I want to travel all over the World too and we are working hard to get there". I smile in acknowledgment, "how cool would that be, I mean being able to travel and play your music wherever you go". John's eyes light up, "that's the plan", then he pauses for a split second before saying again, "yeah that's the plan". John in fairness only has two drinks, he isn't out with me to get drunk, he is genuinely interested in talking to a new person, which I appreciate, as I always enjoy meeting new people as well.

"I'm going to head back to the hotel", John suddenly says, as if realising he's tired, "more travelling tomorrow and more singing to do". "I can't agree more" I reply, "after all, you don't need your voice to get tired either. I will see you again soon and you can let me know how it's all going". John looks a little confused, "great idea Greg, but I'm not sure where I will be, as I'm planning on travelling a lot". I nod, "trust me, we will see each other again, just name the date and I will be there".

John just laughs at me, "what like any date and you'll be there, now that would be freakin' crazy". I look John straight in the eye and answer, "any date John and I will make sure I'm there, the only thing you have to promise me is that we will have a drink together, could be a cup of tea, could be something stronger, your choice, but we must meet". I can tell John thinks this is a crazy idea. Confidently smiling back at John, "well let's test out the theory then". John laughs a slightly nervous laugh, "you're a bit crazy and I like that, but it won't work". "Well", I say, "I believe in everything until it's disproved". John likes my response, "okay agreed", he confirms "I might use that line myself one day". I continue to keep eye contact to show I am serious, "so pick a date then, not the place, just the date". John is still chuckling, "okay... how about we go for a date next year, so in the future but not too long to wait? I have always had a thing for the number nine, like it's my lucky number or something, so let's go for the 9th

February 1961, agreed"? I smile, "that's great and so there is absolutely no doubt let's write this date on a piece of paper, you sign it, I sign it and one of us keeps it as proof". I write the date, sign the paper and pass it to John, who is still not really sure what is happening here. John signs the paper anyway and it's agreed that I will keep it safe. "Well it's great to meet you properly this time and not to spill your tea", I am very much aware that John is more than ready to leave. We shake hands and John leaves to get some much needed sleep. I sit quietly by myself, with another beer, almost pinching myself at chatting properly to the infamous John Lennon, but I also can't believe how well we got on. He certainly has charisma and presence, even before he became a global icon. What a night this turned out to be and one that will go down in the history books of stories that I will never be able to tell anyone! I decide it's a good idea to head back to Tx3, so we can plan my next trip.

Twenty

As I blink from the lights in the room, Annie is standing next to Christian, waiting for my return. "Welcome back, what are the heady days of 1960 like"? Is the sort of stupid question I've began to expect from Christian. "It's a nice place, a lot calmer than these days and people have manners, unlike you of course", came my witty reply. Christian smiles, he seems to like it when I actually have a go back at him, banter I guess. "So what's the plan? What's our next move"? I step towards them, "well that's a really easy question to answer", I reply, "can you send me straight back to the 9th February 1961? Christian can sense the game is on, "of course I can, it will literally take me seconds to program".

Suddenly from the back of the room Ms D Rees speaks up, "but the bigger question is not what date, but where do you need to go? I mean where are we sending you? After all the World is an awfully big place, you could be sent to my favourite place, Las Vegas, or to Brighton as an example". In fairness Ms Rees has raised a very good point and I am slightly embarrassed at my naivety of just assuming Christian would know where to send me. I decide to play this one with a straight bat and apologise for my stupidity, which appears to be the right way of going about this. I then explain the set up, the meeting I had and I show them the piece of paper. Everyone gathers around to look at this unique piece of history and decide it is a great plan that we simply have to follow up. So where the hell is John going to be on the 9th of February 1961?

Christian flips open his lap top, "I'm hoping this is straight forward, if not we can find the answer, but it will take me a little longer". Christian's fingers quickly type into the search engine and then he just stands back, smiling, and groaning, "of course it is, I should have known, it's soo friggin obvious", his face beaming with delight. Annies lack of patience with Christian flares, "Well, come on then, are you going to share"? Christian is thoroughly enjoying the drama and the tension he's creating and laughing as he says slowly, John Lennon, on the 9th of February 1961, was at The Cavern Club, Liverpool". Now I understood why Christian is acting like he is, now it all makes sense, it must be fate!

"Oh boy", is the slightly intimidating sounds that leave my lips. I am incredibly excited to be going to one of the most iconic clubs in the World, but also at a time that isn't just in history, it is literally history in the making and I will be right there! How amazing to be there on this auspicious day and meeting John, who will be right on the cusp of having the World put at his feet. Christian suggests I get change into something more fitting for a visit to the club, whatever that's supposed to mean. I need to wear a nice pair of trousers or they won't let me in apparently. Christian also suggests I arrive around half eleven in the morning, to make sure I find a table in view of the stage and of course the boys. I like to arrive early for all my meetings, but eleven thirty in the morning, sounds ridiculously early to me. Surely they wouldn't be on stage much before eight at night, just as the crowd is getting going. Christian smirks his cocky, don't you know anything kind of smirk. "The Beatles are actually on stage at noon until two in the afternoon, so if you arrive later you will miss

225

them, dope"! Noon for a concert is very early, but hey, what do I know?

After a quick change, like an actor in a show, rushing to get back on stage for the second act, I am ready. Not just ready, but swinging 60's ready, as I am wearing the slickest suit I have ever worn. It's like I am going to a fancy dress party and the theme is the sixties, but this party is about to get very real, very quick. Christian has established how to get me inside a toilet cubicle on arrival, oh the glamour of my job. This way I'd have passed the security door men, but Christian will conveniently place a ticket for that days shows, inside my pocket, just in case I am challenged. The set up is perfect, I just need to deliver the goods now - no pressure there, then.

I stand in my ever familiar spot and I notice Christian is looking a little nervous, which is unusual as he normally doesn't show this, even if he's feeling it. "Everything okay Chris", I ask, as I don't like the way he isn't as settled and as confident as usual. "Yeah, of course" comes his reply, which reassures me ever so slightly, however he quickly follows this with, "well if anything goes wrong it's your life that's lost, not mine". I blink my eyes ready to shoot him a glaring look and I cheekily reply, "cheers dickhead". However, I hear a strange Liverpudlian voice answering back in an echoing room, "who are you calling a dickhead? Dickhead". I just stand still, grinning and shaking my head, Christian has sent me off to the club, without checking I am ready, just so he can get the last word in.

I decide to stand still until the person in the other cubicle leaves, as I don't want a fight before my day has even started. As the man leaves and the door closes, I leave my cubicle and catch sight of myself in the mirror. I'm aware I have a wicked suit on and I have seen I am wearing some pretty fashionable shoes, but what catches me by surprise is my hairstyle, it looks amazing. I have generally kept the same haircut for the last twenty five years, so to see me sporting a new and cool haircut is awesome and I feel all down with the kids.

I leave the toilets high on life and the excitement is building to the point where my stomach has knots in it. As I round the corner, I am quickly greeted by how small the club is, how low the ceilings are and strangely how empty the place is. I was expecting the club to be big and bouncing full with people, screaming at the bands on the stage. It is however quiet, maybe fifty or so people mulling around. I glance at my watch which displays eleven thirty four and I head for the bar to order a beer. I can see a few ladies entering through the main doors and decide to get to a table ready for the main event of the day, the main event for me anyway.

The group strut on to the stage at exactly noon and I give a quick whoop and a clap, which no one else does. John and Paul don't even look up, as they are pulling the guitar straps over their heads, ready to play. The lights suddenly beam onto the stage and I can tell they can't see the crowd, or the lack of it. The group for what it's worth look incredible in their black leather jackets and leather trousers. They start to play and settle into a rhythm of songs, the odd joke and banter with the crowd and then a few more songs. After about an hour I decide to head back to the bar for another beer and as I return to my seat, John casually announces, "the next song is for a friend of mine, Greg, who I've spotted in the crowd today". What a buzz, of course no one knows who Greg is, or that it is me, but I could die a very happy man, right here and now. The show seems to come and go and the crowd warm to them nicely as they become more relaxed and show their personalities. It's a privilege to have been here and they have certainly improved since the last time I saw them, earlier in the day for me of course.

Once the show ends, they disappear off stage and John comes out to find me, for a drink and a catch up. "Hey man", is his cool opening line, "how are you doing"? "You look great", I tell him, "you've improved a bit then", I chuckle at him. John isn't sure if I am saying they were really bad last time or if they are just better now, but accepts the compliment anyway. "So what the hell are you doing here", John is intrigued. "Well after seeing an average sounding support act in Scotland, I thought I'd see an average sounding group in Liverpool for a change". John laughs and slaps me on my arm, "it's great to see you Greg, so what have you been up to"? I am genuinely happy to see John, "Oh this and that and keeping an eye on your career in between. More importantly, you know why I'm here, right"? John suddenly goes a bit quiet and shoots me a strange look. "I can't remember what date we wrote on that paper Greg, honestly, but if you're telling me that it's today, then I'm gonna freak out". John leans towards me in anticipation, as I casually place my hand into my jacket pocket and pull out the piece of paper. John smiles, a nervous smile, "open it, go on", he encourages. I unfold the paper, as cool as I can and slide it across the table towards him. John's eyes quickly flicker over it, reading the date - 9th February 1961. John glances back at me quickly and then again at the paper, looking at his signature on it next to mine and slowly leans back in his chair. "Woooah", is all he says, like he is having an epiphany. "So how the friggin hell did you know, when we last met, that I would be right here today"? I lean in again, to speak quieter with John and he reciprocates. "John, time is an amazing thing, time can be the slowest or it can be the quickest thing in your life, but it's the one thing that should never be taken for granted. Time is more precious than gold, or money and it's the one thing everyone has too little of. My job is to show you how time can be grasped forever and in doing so, you can have all the time in World. You will not understand this, but the last time I saw you in Scotland, it was earlier this morning for me. Several months have past for you, but I've not even had lunch in between". John is sitting still, listening intently and is struggling to process what he is hearing, but interestingly he doesn't laugh at me, or tell me I'm mad. Instead he asks some intelligent questions about how it is even possible, what year have I travelled from and the best question of all, why am I meeting him? I try to answer every question, one at a time and as honestly as I can, but I am very conscious not to tell him anything about his death, or the date of his death. John is brilliantly articulate in his questioning, his disbelief and eventually his conclusion, that I am either telling him the truth or I am a very good liar. After we talk for about three hours, John eventually admits he is beaten, his brain hurts and he needs to get some sleep. John explains his busy schedule to me and how they are booked to play nearly every day, for the next two months. I decide not to push him any further today, but ask him to think about what I've been saying and how I believe he can benefit from joining up with us. I agree to meet John for breakfast in the morning, before they head off to Aintree, apparently.

As John swaggers off back stage, he genuinely looks a little confused and shaken up, which, if I'm honest gives me a strange sense of power. I continue to sit here to enjoy another beer, as the crowds pour in for more musical acts of the day. I suddenly realise, I am sat alone once again for a business meeting. It doesn't seem to matter what my job is, or where I am in the World, I always seem to be sitting in a cafe, or bar. I decide to head for a hotel, to sleep and freshen up, ahead of my morning meeting with John. No sooner have I checked myself in, I sit on the bed exhausted from the day and I am quickly sound asleep.

It is still dark when I wake and as I check my watch, it displays six eleven. I have a shower then gather my things together and leave for John's hotel, located about a ten minute walk from nine. I enter the lobby area shortly after seven and sit down waiting for John to arrive. The humour of not knowing what time he could arrive, is not lost on me. John eventually arrives at half past seven and he doesn't look like he's slept that much. "Good morning", I announce to him, a lot louder in the quiet echoing lobby, than I had planned it to be. "Thank God you're hear", is John's unexpected response, "I've been up most of the night trying to get my head around everything you said last night. I even wondered if I'd dreamt it all, or I'd gone mad and made it all up". I smile at John, my caring smile and suggest, "shall we walk and talk"? John agrees and also highlights that there could be a song somewhere in that statement.

As we stroll around the streets of Liverpool, I am able to answer more burning questions that John poses. I explain "you can live your life as you see fit, we are not here to govern your life, this is just about us being with you, at the end of your life. When time has run out, we will be right with you, to get you into the future, for your next exciting chapter to begin". John processes this information fairly quickly, but asks, "what happens to my body, does it just vanish"? I reassure, "the exact split second you die, you are pulled from your body. Think of your body as a capsule, which you no longer need. Your "actual" body will remain there, lifeless as you have already left that time any anyone who is with your body will not see any difference. Your "spirit" for want of a better word, will arrive with us in the future, instantly and you'll look exactly the same". John, as anyone would, struggles to fully understand this and can't stop laughing at me. He follows this by stating, "this is completely mad", but in the end he admits that he is interested. "This doesn't mean I will do it though", he repeats, "but I am very interested". I am happy with this level of commitment at this stage, after all this is mind blowing information. I am also fully aware of how far we have come since yesterday.

John decides to leave the discussion alone for now, comfortable that he has taken this as far as he wants to right now. "There is still one thing that is bothering me though, why me", he asks? "What does my future hold, that makes me an attraction to you? I answer John as honestly as I can, without giving too much away. After all, if I had told him The Beatles will become the biggest group of all time, that would ruin the ride for him. My response is therefore, "yes The Beatles will be successful, but the line up will be different to what you have today".

Before I leave, John says, "look Greg, I trust what you've told me, but I am going to need more proof, you understand though, right"? In fairness, if I were in John's shoes, I'm pretty sure I'd be the same. John asks, "can you pick another date to meet up again, maybe a memorable one, but this time I want proof in advance". As embarrassing as this is, I am only really aware of two dates in the history of The Beatles. The obvious one, being the date John Lennon died, which clearly wouldn't work here and the second being the 5th of October 1962. To put this into context, this is the date The Beatles release their first single, but I only know this because it is also the day before the James Bond film, "Dr No" is released. This is a classic pub quiz question, which is the only reason I know it.

I therefore plump for the 5th of October 1962, as the next date to meet up. John's face lights up with excitement and immediately agrees to the date. "But what happens on this date? As I said, I need to have proof in advance this time". I reluctantly tell John, "this is the date you will release your first single as a group, but I'm not going to say anymore than that". John looks like a child at Christmas, "agreed", he answers, tapping his nose. I continue, "wherever you are on October the fifth, I need you to leave my name as "Mickey Mouse", on the guest list for my back stage pass, or it will be impossible to get near you". John is still beaming at the fact they will be releasing a single into the charts! "Yes of course I can do that for you", he says, writing the date in his notebook that he carries everywhere with him, right next to his scribbles of Mickey Mouse. "Just one more thing before you go", John says, "if you can truly time travel I want you to do it today, I mean today your time of course". I nod all smug, "of course I can do that" and with that response, John stabs a fork into the middle of my hand. I immediately shout, "Holy shit", at the top of my voice. The pain is a burning, shock inducing pain, that seems to travel at the speed of light, all the way to my heart. I am in agony, as John pulls the fork back out again and immediately apologises to me. "What the hell did you do that for you knob", comes tumbling out of my mouth. Again another classic moment in my history of saying the wrong thing, to these iconic people. John explains, "I'm so sorry, but this will be the proof I'm looking for, after all, if you show up with these fresh fork marks in your hand, at our next meeting, then it will be proof that this happened on the same day for you, today that is". I immediately understand why he has done it, but it doesn't stop me wanting to punch him in the face. As I am in so much pain, I agree to say our goodbyes quickly and meet him again later, or as it will be for John, on the 5th of October 1962, with a bloody, fork marked hand. As I leave John, I hurry to get myself quickly out of sight, to ensure no one else sees me disappear. With this excruciating pain, I immediately trigger the boomerang. Like every other time, I am instantly back with Annie and Christian, who are shocked at my blood stained return.

"What have you done", Annie immediately challenges me, looking straight at my hand. "I had a fight with a fork and lost", is the only thing I can say, through my gritted teeth. Annie rushes over to me, which in that split second, I think is a very nice and caring thing to do. However, as she stands in front of me, Annie immediately asks, "but has the job been ruined"? With blood dripping onto the floor, I quickly glance at Christian, who I can see rolling his eyes in disbelief. My response to Annie is strained, as I confirm, "no Annie, everything is still in tact and the fact that I have blood gushing out of my hand, is strangely proof that everything is going to plan". Annie is clearly relieved to hear the update and immediately starts to back peddle, "sorry Greg, of course I am very concerned about you as well and we will need to get you all fixed up urgently". I am in more pain than I have ever experienced in my lifetime, but, "I don't want to be fixed up", is my response, which upon reflection, is a little snappy. I continue in a calmer voice, "I really need to get back to John urgently, as the whole fork in hand, blood dripping things is the plan". Everyone looks at me confused, as I've clearly not explained myself very well. Despite the pain I walk them through the events and how I have ended up with a fork in my hand. Christian immediately understands and is already a few steps ahead of everyone else, which impresses me. He might appear to be a jack the lad, but in fact he know his job inside out and the experience he's gained over the years, means he is able to process this sort of information incredibly quickly. "So what date are we searching for this time"? he asks, clearly keen on not wasting anymore time, as he realises I need to get back to John quickly. In a wincing voice, I confirm, "5th of October 1962, but I have no idea where".

Christian is immediately at his system, typing away in the search engine frantically. "Leave it to me", he confirms, before quickly following this with "Nuneaton". Looking at him, "I have no idea where Nuneaton is, I assume it's in the U.K"? Christian chortles, "yes it's in England, near Birmingham, but I am working on connecting The Beatles to that place and date. Give me a second, there got it", he announces proudly. "Let's get you back there and inside the co-operative hall where they are playing yet another gig. Looking at this list of venues and dates they played at that time, they must be exhausted". I smile, with a sarcastic reply of, "hmm I don't know what that feels like". As Christian is setting the systems up, I ask, "can you get me into the hall around the time they come off stage, I'm not sure I want to see another Beatles gig and I really do need to get this hand seen to. I need to be in and out of there as quickly as I can this time". Christian nods, "absolutely", followed quickly with, "it's done and you're ready to go". I quickly get myself into position as Christian asks, "are you ready"? I quickly nod confirmation back as I am eager to get on with this. Then as before I am back in 1962, with music blaring in the distance. Yet again I arrive in the elegance of a smelly toilet cubicle, just as someone opens the door and lets in the flood of music that is coming from the group on stage. The noise from the crowd this time is electrifying and a part of me now wishes I'd arrived earlier to enjoy the concert, this is by far the best atmosphere I've felt from all the gigs I have seen them play. I pull open the door with my good hand to leave the toilets and I can hear Paul saying goodbye to the crowd. So instead of heading towards the stage, I head towards back stage and a big burly looking security guard. "Hi, how you doing"? is my best attempt at sounding cool. The man just stares at me, clearly annoyed by the number of people trying to sneak backstage. "Hi I'm Greg and John is expecting me", the man rolls his eyes, before stating in a very matter of fact voice, "yeah of course he is"! "No he is, my other name is Mickey Mouse", I say with a huge cheesy grin. The security guard immediately changes his attitude and apologises, while opening the door at the same time. "I'm so sorry sir, you'll find Mr Lennon in the third door on your right as you head down this corridor". Peering around the door, "thank you", I confidently reply, "now please make sure no one else gets through here". I quickly find myself outside a red door, with a white sheet of paper sellotaped to it and John Lennon handwritten in marker pen on it. I knock on the door and hear John's dulcet tones, requesting me to enter. I push open the door and smile at him, as I cross into his threshold. John immediately jumps out his chair and greets me with a hot sweaty hug. "Sorry man", he says in a quiet voice, "I've just come off stage, I wasn't sure if you'd show up tonight, how the hell have you been"? "Well considering I only saw you about half an hour ago, my time of course, when you stabbed a friggin fork into my hand, I'm still in absolute agony". I lift my hand to show John my blood stained hand, with four perfect dots, wincing, I ask, "is that enough proof"? John stumbles slightly, before sitting down in a chair, "shiiiiit", is all he says, then "shiiiiit", once more. John is struggling to piece it all together, then suddenly laughs out loud and points to my suit, "you're still wearing the same bloody suit as well". I glance at my outfit, then back at John, "Well of course I am, I retort, it's not like I've had time to change is it"? John is blown away by the realisation of it all, then changes to an apologetic, "shit man, I stabbed a friggin fork into your hand". Still wincing I stumble slightly, as it's all getting pretty painful now and I really need to get my hand seen to. John's concern level rises and he suggests calling for help, which I agree with, as the pain is becoming unbearable. I sit in John's chair, exhausted and in pain, when a young man arrives to check out my hand. "That looks nasty", I overhear him say to John, "we need to get him to a hospital quickly". The man also looks suspiciously at John, "how the hell did it happen", John in fairness looks guilty as charged but says, "some young thug in the crowd did it", swiftly followed by "what is the World coming to eh"?

A few minutes later I am being bundled into a car and driven to a nearby hospital for treatment. John kindly checks me in and a doctor comes to look at my hand, all in a short space of time. In next to no time I'm cleaned up and drugged up, to take away my pain and John stays with me throughout. As I am starting to feel better, John apologises again, which I brush off with, "well in fairness, if I was in your position I would have stabbed me as well", which is about all I can think to say.

John sits next to my hospital bed and with a boyish smile, tells me, "we released our first single today", which by his tone is intended to be clearly stating the obvious. He continues, "I wrote this date in my notebook, next to the name Mickey Mouse and I've looked at them every day since I last saw you. I've often wondered if you'd really turn up, or if I would end up disappointed by the end of today. Then like an angel you appeared and still carrying the injuries I gave you, but I'm still not really sure what the hell you want from me"?

"Listen John, we want you, your brain and your talent but we don't want any of that until you die. Like I said the last time we met, you can live your life exactly as you please, but when the time comes for you to die, we will be there to collect you at that exact moment. You will just appear with me on the other side, ready to start your new life with us". John stares into space for a second, before asking, "that really does sound truly amazing, but what's the catch"? I lower my eyebrows, "John, there is no catch, no charge, just us making sure we don't lose you, when your time comes". John seems relieved, "I think I'm sold on the idea, after all what have I got to lose"? I am certainly relieved, "exactly John", I say, "and I will be there to greet you when it's time. If you are up for it, I will send my people to meet you, they will introduce themselves as working for Tx3 and they will get you sorted". John is staring at me, it's like he is staring right through me, "so you're saying I can't die, because the moment I die, I actually arrive somewhere in the future and can carry on living again". I'm impressed with his way of looking at this, before confirming, "well, when you put it that way, yes you are absolutely right".

I stare intently at John, then blurt out, "Time my friend is short for everyone, time is very precious and no matter how much money you make, we all crave more time with loved ones, more time to just live. No amount of money can buy you more time.

No matter if you are rich or poor, famous or not, when the end comes, we are all the same, we all wish we'd had more time to be with the people we love".

John sighs a reflective sigh, "I'm almost certain I'm in, but why me, it's not like I have anything to give to the future generations"? I clearly need to give him a bit more detail, if I am going to convince him, "John, the reason you have been chosen, is because of what you are yet to achieve. I am from sixty years in the future, so I know what you go on to achieve in the coming years. You and Paul will forever be cemented in history, you need to find your own path, live your own life and just imagine what you can do to influence the World, when the time is right of course". I deliberately decide to quote his own, as yet not written, lyrics in the hope of sparking a connection, "John, just imagine all the people and how you can drive them to want a better life. Maybe I'm a dreamer, but I'm not the only one and I hope someday you will join us"? John holds up his finger, to stop me talking, as he quickly scribbles my words into his notepad, before stating, "That's brilliant, I'm going to work on that for a song"!

"John, you need to go, you have work to do. Today's a big day for you, after all it's not everyday you get to release your first single, is it? I bet you need to promote it and please make time to celebrate it. Remember, time goes by too quickly, so savour every precious moment that you can". John stands to leave, "so will I see you again"? I smile back, "you just try stopping me", I eagerly reply. "I will be back, but I need you to seriously think about everything I've said". Pulling the handle on the door, John acknowledges, "I'm pretty sure I'm in Greg, but you're right, it's a big decision, I need a little more time to consider everything". I gesture him to leave, "that's all I can ask for, now go and enjoy your life and I will come back on a 9th February, as the 9th has worked for us, hasn't it"? John smiling a cheeky smile, opens his book, to write down 9th of February, then he looks up and asks, "how about 1964? I mean the 9th February 1964, are you happy with that"? I nod in agreement, "that's about eighteen months from now, by then you'll see how your career is going, which will help you decide how you feel about all this". John grins, "okay, then that's a date, I wonder where we will meet, but wherever it is, I will make sure to leave a pass for my favourite Mickey Mouse"! I practically force him out the door, "thanks buddy, now go and enjoy your first single, release day".

John turns to leave, pauses to glance back at me shaking his head, as if in disbelief at everything that has happened, then quietly pulls the door shut behind him. I am suddenly alone, in a hospital bed, without any pain, thanks to the drugs they've provided, but with a great big bandage on my hand.

I am resting peacefully when I suddenly wonder how the hell am I supposed to explain this injury to Bonnie. I am supposed to be working in a boring office job, where a fork being stabbed into your hand doesn't happen. I need to invent a mad client or something, or I could just stay here for a few weeks until it healed? The second option doesn't really appeal, after all Bonnie and myself are just starting to work things out. Deep down I know I need to head back home and take a little time off, with my family. It feels like an awfully long time since I'd seen Bonnie and the twins, but of course it was only this morning really, even though I've been travelling for days. This time travelling shit is enough to mess with my brain. I climb out of bed and steady myself next to it. Without any further thought, I trigger the boomerang. In an instant I am stood in front of the others, with my bandaged hand and a list of things to update them on.

Twenty One

A debrief follows with the team, followed by a
check over by the medical team, who are
apparently located in the building for safety
reasons. I am quickly given the all clear and the
doctors are patronisingly surprised at how well the
doctors in the 1960's have patched me up. I am
also given some medication to last the next week,
while my hand heals and I am pretty much sent on
my way. I play on the incredibly busy time I've
had on this case and tell the team I am going to
have a few days off, to recover. I feel like I need to
justify the time off, but in fairness Annie doesn't

even blink an eye and just says, "you need to make time to relax so enjoy your break". So that's it, I'm done and on my way home for a week of no work, happy days. During my drive home I realise I am exhausted, which, let's be honest is crazy, as I haven't been doing the job for long. So how can I be experiencing burn out already? But hey I can take as much time off work as I need to, so I am going to enjoy this break.

As I arrive back home, I quietly open the front door and can hear the house alive with family noises. I shout, "I'm home" and the twins come running up to greet me, quickly followed with questions about my hand. This draws attention to Bonnie who also comes to see what all the fuss is about. "How the hell did you do that", is the question I've been dreading. I reply with the obvious response, "well, a very long and boring story cut short, there was a crazy client in the office who, for some bizarre reason stabbed a fork into my hand". Bonnie looks genuinely concerned, "why the hell would someone do that", she screeches, "ahh because he is completely mad and also because he believes we owe him money, which he clearly needs treatment for. It was all sorted out very quickly, he was arrested and taken away. The report we had back, says he has done this before. So listen, as dramatic as it sounds, I've had it checked out and I have been give some medication to help with the pain. The doctors also prescribed a couple of other things :

One, I must have the rest of this week off work to relax and recover.

Two, I must spend time with my family, eating out and playing.

And three, apparently I need to be massaged by someone who's name begins with the letter B".

Bonnie immediately rolls her eyes at me, "look", I say apologetically, "it's come straight from the doctor this time, so doctors orders and all that". Bonnie smiles back at me, "well Mr Smarty Pants :

One, I'm sure you can have the time off work, after all you wouldn't have been hurt if you weren't in work, so that's the least they can do for you.

Two, you can take the kids to a football party tonight, so you can tick the spending time with the family box, but we can't eat out as they will be eating there.

And three, the massage". Now this is the part where I pretend I'm all masculine and it doesn't really matter when Bonnie creates an excuse, but in truth I'm hurt, with her constant excuses not to make time for us to play, like we used to do. Bonnie continues, "the massage will have to wait until later". Bonnie however, gives me a hug and whispers in my ear, "much later, when the kids have gone to bed". I gulp so uncontrollably loud, that I am immediately embarrassed and feel like an excited teenager all over again. Maybe getting a fork stabbed into my hand is the best way to get sex, who'd have known? A massage later, when the twins are sleeping, is like music to my ears, and it definitely puts a spring back in my step.

I take the twins to their friends party and sit chatting with the other parents about their children and their life's problems. Parties are much more interesting these days, having a good chat and a cup of tea in hand, as the twins just go and play. For me it's nice to hear about other people's lives and in fairness I realised a long time ago, that we are all pretty similar. We all have our struggles in life, be it financially or emotionally, we are all just trying to get by. Interestingly the richer the people, the more unhappy they appear to be. It's as if the more money you have, the more money you spend, meaning the more money you need to earn again, like some vicious hamster wheel.

As we drive home, the twins both start to speak at the same time again, occasionally pausing for me to answer "yes", or "no". I love listening to them and this new job allows me the time to be with them, unlike my last job, where I was always working. Arriving home, we carry out the usual ritual we do every time we've been to a party. The twins run into the house and empty their party bags, all over the table, letting the plastic party crap all fall out. They look for the sweets and lollipops and eat them, like it is their first time to eat anything sugary. However, with time ticking away and school tomorrow, I am eager to get them into bed and off to sleep. I put on the TV and tell the twins they have ten minutes to watch something, before bed. All is going to plan, until I hear a sudden, "whoosh", sound as I turn around just in time to catch the last lumps of sick coming out, quickly followed by a scream for "muuuuum". It is at this point I know instantly that my plans for tonight are ruined, as I trundle off to find some cleaning gear. As I start scrubbing the floor and heaving at the smell, Bonnie moves the twins up to bed. I can hear lots of movement upstairs as they slowly settle and eventually there is silence.

The next morning I awake to the sound of more whooshing going into the toilet and Bonnie frantically shouting, "Greg can you get out of bed and come help"! What is this fresh hell that I have woken up to? The next 20 minutes are messy and certainly not the way anyone should be awoken. But things quickly settle down and it becomes apparent that my day of relaxing around the house is out the window. In fairness this is how the next few days go, until Saturday morning when the sickness bug has finally gone and the carnage of football training and play dates, ensue once more.

Both Bonnie and myself are exhausted from the week, despite neither of us going into work. We took turns with the cuddling and nurse type duties, followed by trips to the shops and the pharmacy, with the occasional cooking of meals thrown in for good measure. In between all of the sickness duties, Bonnie and myself managed to have a chat about life, the twins and her job. Bonnie has decided to quit her job and move on to something else. At this particular time Bonnie likes the idea of being at home looking after the twins and enjoying life and I am happy to support this.

This morning I wake fresh for the day around eight o'clock and it's a gloriously sunny Sunday morning. I lean over to Bonnie to give her a kiss and I can feel the warmth escaping from her as I snuggled into her bottom and curled legs. What a great way to start the day. I am determined to have a calm and enjoyable last day off work and soon head downstairs to make pancakes for breakfast.

The twins come running down shortly after me and put the TV on, as I finish the cooking. As much as life can be a bit crap sometimes, all in all it isn't that bad really. I need to remind myself that we have a lovely, healthy family, a nice house with a garden for the twins to play, food in the cupboards and a well paid job. There are plenty of people out there that don't have these things and of course the secret cherry on the top, is the fact I can now time travel, which means I am able to meet these amazing people. My mind quickly drifts back to my John Lennon case and what will be the next steps? I am due back at work tomorrow, heading back to meet John and hopefully to get things wrapped up. Although I feel a slight sense of sadness that my time meeting John in different places, is coming to an end. If John agrees to sign up, it will mean an end of the road for me, he will then transfer to the team and history will play out his death. I guess I will be able to meet and visit this legend of a man, a man I now think of as a friend, but time with him will be different and indeed shorter after all this. I pause, "wow I'm friends with John Lennon", mind you I am not sure if John feels the same way, I'd like to think so, but I wouldn't like to be so presumptuous. The silence and my thoughts are suddenly broken by the noise of the house coming alive, with the twins arguing over a game and I am immediately back in the real World. I sit with them, while they eat their breakfast and I look for compliments, as I am convinced these are the nicest pancakes they have ever eaten. Our leisurely breakfast suddenly turns into a mad rush to get them ready for a Sunday morning club, that I'd forgotten about. This is followed by lunch and heading back out to a friends birthday party. Taxi dad strikes again and before I know it, I am back in bed, snuggling under the covers and drifting off to sleep.

Twenty Two

The alarm seems to be laughing at me yet again, like it is enjoying waking me up on a very wet, windy and cold Monday morning. If you ever need to provide a photograph of the day "Monday", then the weather outside perfectly sums it up today. I however, am not feeling down or moody, I feel excited to be going back to work. I am ready to get back to the project, but I am also more than ready to leave the house, after a week of sickness. I will be heading back to meet old friends and in all reality, to have a mini break of my own, which I really need after this past week of sickness. So waking up on a cold and wet Monday isn't a negative for me, it's a definite positive.

I shower, dress and head downstairs to see everyone, before leaving for work. The house is pretty calm and organised today, as Bonnie has everything perfectly under control. I give everyone my usual goodbye hugs and kisses and head out the front door, into the cold and wet morning. I sit in my car, watching its theatre play out in front of me, as I start her up. The initial mood lights to set the scene, followed by the exciting dashboard greetings and then the eventual roar of the orchestrated throaty engine, as the theatre of it all climaxes. "God I love this car", I mutter out loud. I wonder if I love it just a little too much, as if my relationship with a lump of metal isn't a healthy one? I scroll through the music in my music app and stop at The Beatles. What a perfect way to start the day and my inevitable journey back to Tx3. As I pull off the driveway, onto the road I feel alive and at peace with myself. Life has been a long journey to this point, but all those experiences have put me in a good place to deal with the different people I meet. I am at one with myself, like I've arrived and this is how life is meant to be.

My rain filled drive to work is an enjoyable one, singing loudly like I am actually in the band. My role in the band is to sing the harmonies and I think I do a decent job. For the people in their cars around me, I probably sound awful and probably look like an idiot, but I don't care. As I approach Tx3, I turn the music right down so I can arrive calm and in control. I hope John has spent the last eighteen months seriously thinking about this opportunity and that the fame hasn't made him think he is invincible. I am all too much aware of the pressure to get the right result here, in fact there is only one result that is really acceptable. I stop my car and, as usual, I am greeted with a friendly, "good morning sir", which I really like. As I enter the building, in all its glorious wonder, Ms Rees approaches me smiling. "I bet you're looking forward to today aren't you"? "Well actually, yes I am, we are getting to the sharp end of things now, but I am keen to deliver for you and the whole team", I quickly reply. Ms Rees, smiles a forced smile at me, "I'm pleased you're ready to deliver, this is a very important mission for the success of Tx3 and we can't afford to mess it up". I suddenly feel exposed, that dreaded pressure to deliver feeling, returning once again, which is not good for me. Ms Rees calmly and quietly points out that, "failure is not an option here" and encourages me to not accept a no, should I be presented with one. I confidently, stop in the corridor in an attempt to take back the power. I too smile and whisper, "trust me Ms Rees, I have no intention of letting you or the team down, I've invested too heavily in this". Then casually walk away and towards Christian's room, while suddenly being conscious of every flat footed step I make, as my legs become heavy. As I open the door I am relieved, as I've made it without falling over, but I am immediately

shocked, as the room is full of people, all
apparently waiting for me!

Twenty Three

I quickly glance around at the various faces and only recognise a few, including Annie and the amazing John F Kennedy. It's at this point I realise just how important, this very important job, is. My brain is screaming expletives at me, while I try to convey calmness personified and probably fail. The noise of chatter and excitement fills the air and Christian catches my eye, he is looking awkward and apologetic at the sight that greets me. It is like he is telepathically trying to say he is sorry about all this, like he has only just found out about all this himself. Almost certainly a plea coming from his face, to say he would have warned me had he known, but he had no clue either. I simply wink at him, to try and show I understand and to confirm we are a team here. I know I need Christian now more than ever and amongst all these faces, he is probably the only one, that I truly trust. Christian doesn't do politics, he plays it straight, he just wants to win and that is good enough for me.

Annie steps forward, out from the group and the chatter quickly silences, as the others all look in my direction. "Good morning Greg", booms Annie's voice across the room, like we are the best of friends. I quite like Annie but I certainly couldn't consider her a friend, as I am not that presumptuous. Annie is without doubt my boss and the person who hired me, so this strange accent in her voice only increases my uneasiness. Annie continues, using theatrical arms, "everyone, this is Greg", it is very unsettling as everyone claps for me. "Thank you", is all I can say, as I nod like I am some sort of royal dignitary. Annie quickly takes hold of my arm and manoeuvres me to introduce a few people. These people are apparently investors in the company or they are connected to the company in some capacity. Then Annie introduces me to a youngish, fairly chubby man with glasses. "This is Mark, he's on secondment from the CIA, I think I mentioned him to you the other day". Mark appears quite intense so I shake his hand, smile and confirm, "Annie has indeed mentioned you to me. Annie says you'll be with us for a short time". Mark nods, "yes a short time, but I'm not sure how long yet, could be my last day today, it just depends on where my services are required and when really". I try to appear interested, but in reality I couldn't give two hoots for how long Mark is staying, or his role, as I am just concerned about getting on with my day and of course the job in hand. As I glance around the room, Christian is gesturing me towards him. "Well it's nice to meet you Mark", I say, "but I need to check in with

Christian". Annie smiles acceptance of my leaving and I walk towards Christian pulling faces, like I need to get out of here. A tall, skinny looking man walks towards me, with his hand offered out, but to my relief he just continues straight past, saying a friendly, "good morning Mr Chapman". I am certainly relieved he doesn't want to speak with me, as I reach Christian. "What the friggin hell is going here", I ask. Christian is already flapping his hands, shushing me and smiling through gritted teeth. "I didn't know about the welcome party either, but what I do know is we need to get you ready and pretty quickly. We have completed the debrief and everything you need is ready to go. Just focus on the job in hand, so we can get you away to 1964, without any issues please".

I am very happy to oblige and quickly leave the main room to change into the clothes assigned for me. As I am finishing getting ready, Christian joins me, "you're going to the 9th February 1964, The

Beatles have enjoyed a good amount of success and you'll be heading to the U.S.A". I liked the states the last time I was there, albeit for a different job, "but where exactly am I going"? Christian gives me his usually cocky smile, "you will meet them at the side of a stage, just before they go on, for their very first, Ed Sullivan Show. I can get you in the right spot, so you can say hi to John, you can then watch from the sidelines and hopefully catch up with him afterwards". I am excited, "I get to go all the way to the states quicker than Concorde had ever made it and back again for that matter". We then enter the main room once more and Christian veers off to his system, to get things ready. Everyone stops to stare at me, like I am an astronaut walking towards the shuttle. I literally feel time slowing, I'm convinced I'm actually walking in slow motion, like the perfect movie sequence. Everyone is smiling and pointing at me and I suddenly realise how people like John Lennon must feel, like being a fish in a great big fish bowl with no escape and I don't like it. I make my way to my usual place and as I turn to face Christian, everyone is being ushered further away. Amongst all the background noise, I can't really hear anything, which is very off putting. I try to focus on the job, but it is like an out of body experience. Christian is standing in his usual spot, but instead of calm, quietness, there is a constant noise, so our usual chat about me being ready can't happen this time. I take a deep breath and lock eyes with Christian, as he is the one controlling the systems and I want to see his direction. He smiles an uncomfortable smile and shows me his hand and five fingers, quickly changing to four, three, two and one index finger glaring at me, as I nod back to him. Instantly the strange atmosphere and noise changes and I am suddenly engulfed with live music, a cheering crowd and TV cameras everywhere. I am stood to the side of a stage, right beside a great tall, red, curtain.

Twenty Four

I have arrived but feel exhausted, not from the trip, but the sheer attention received back at Tx3 and I am relieved to be away from there. A quick surveillance of the area and I can see people rushing around all over the place, all looking very important and no one is taking any notice of me, which is great. As I turn to look behind me, the boys are walking in my direction, along with a man I don't recognise carrying a guitar. John spots me instantly and his face lights up like a glitter ball as he approaches. Paul however, reaches me first and genuinely looks pleased to see me, "hey man", he says, "you look great, John said you'd be coming today, so glad you could make it". With that he pats my shoulder and carries on walking past. John approaches with his arms open wide and we give each other a decent friendly man hug. "Hey.. how are you", John asks? "I told everyone you'd be here today and look, here you are. Amazing and you're here to see us on the Ed Sullivan Show, you were absolutely right, the 9th February has been a great date for us". I am over the moon to be in John's company again, "but where is George"? I ask as the strange man walks past me. John is suddenly being ushered onto the stage before he can answer, "gotta go man, catch up when we're done yeah"? I nod, as he has already been pulled too far away from me, to hear any reply I might give.

As I stand to the side of the stage, watching their interview, I am impressed with how polished they have become. They look great in their suits and their floppy hair, which is clearly very different in this era. They are very funny, intriguing and clearly loving the moment. It's a pleasure to witness them at the top of their powers. The sct they play is also mind numbingly brilliant and I now understand all the hype. After the show is "in the can", I overhear someone saying, they are headed back in my direction and they are clearly very happy with how it has all gone. I greet them once again and John and I head off to his private room for drinks and a catch up. I am expecting a raucous occasion, with alcohol celebrations, but John is very content with a cup of tea, which I join him with. John takes off his sweaty jacket and then looks at me intently. "You don't look a day older than the last time I saw you", he smirks. I giggle and show him my hand which is still a little sore, "it's starting to heal quite nicely now". John looks concerned, "oh man, I am genuinely so sorry, I'd forgotten about that, but I'm glad you're getting better".

John tells me how the last year or so has been for him and the group. They are constantly on the road, but all the hard work is now paying off. He continues, "I've been looking forward to today for a very long time, wondering where exactly we would be meeting up. Then a few months ago the plans started to take shape and we were told we would be here. I just knew today would be great, this is definitely our special date now". I grin at him, I've missed John and I've missed listening to his stories. It never really matters what he says, it is just great being in his company. During a pause in the chat I seize my moment, "so what are your thoughts about Tx3 now John? do you think you'll be joining us on this fascinating journey"? John beams the most amazing smile I think I have ever seen from him, "What do you think"? Looking me right in the eye, "I've not stopped thinking about it. In a way, I've had today in my mind as the deadline day. I need to have this all sorted now, as it's taken up a lot of space in my head. I've moved from a no, don't be stupid man, to a yeah why the hell not. I eventually came to a final decision over Christmas and I'm in. You only live once right? So I want to make that one chance last as long as possible, so yeah, I'm definitely in". I'm so relieved to hear this and it certainly takes a weight off my shoulders as well, with all the pressure being applied back at base. However, I am more relieved to know my friend will be staying with us for a lot longer than the World really knows. The benefits to Tx3 will be huge, but the benefit to me, knowing I can see him after his death is the cherry on top of the cream, on top of the cake! Like Elvis, or Aron as he's called now, I will be able to continue my relationship with John, when we are back home. "That's just brilliant news", I manage to splutter out, with a tear in my eye, "when you arrive, when it's your time of course, I will be there waiting to welcome you, I promise. I appreciate there will be a lot going through your mind at that very moment, but I will be there to welcome you to the other side, so look out for me". John's eyes well up, which catches me by surprise. "Man, I've been worried that I wouldn't make it to today, to give you my answer I mean and it's such a relief to know it's done. I've been having nightmares about something happening to me before today and although I had made my decision, if I couldn't confirm it to you, then I'd have been screwed". "It's all done now John", I warmly reply, "you can go and enjoy your life knowing it's done. Go and be the best you, that you can be", is the best spiritual line I can come up with. I explain to John how it will work from here, how he'd get a visit and they will introduce themselves as coming from Tx3. John looks exhausted and I am convinced this isn't just from all the constant touring they are doing, but from the stress that I have put on him to make this decision. Surely if anyone is presented with this offer, the answer has to be yes, but then again I haven't needed to make that decision! I soon say my goodbyes and we hug a genuine friendship hug goodbye. Then smiling my best smile at John, I instigate the boomerang and leave him in 1964.

I wonder what his reaction will be at seeing me literally disappear right in front of his own eyes? I don't have time to dwell on this thought though, as I am back in the room, the noisy chaotic room, with an instant cheer and clapping being sent around the room. It is like I have just performed the greatest magic trick they have ever seen. I suppose, in all reality, they have just witnessed a man disappear in front of them and then reappear seconds later, which must look pretty amazing. I immediately see Annie and nod confirmation to her that it is all done. Then to Christian, to double confirm as I step towards them. The room suddenly changes into complete silence and all eyes turn from me to Annie, as she clears her throat to make a short speech. "Ladies and gentlemen, what Greg has been able to achieve is incredibly valuable for us all here at Tx3, but invaluable for our future generations. Please take a short break and when you return, we will ask you to stand at the other side of this glass wall, as we want to welcome our guest into a calm environment. But ladies and gentlemen, today we will be welcoming the one and only, Mr John Lennon". The clapping starts once again and then the crowd start to disperse.

I am suddenly alone with Annie, Christian and Ms Rees, who require the usual debrief. I feel proud of my work and proud to be a part of this team. Annie is incredibly pleased with the success of today and confirms she has just given the order to the repat team, who will get John ready to be received. Annie then turns a little serious, "Greg we need you here to welcome Mr Lennon, as you did for your last John". I am confused by this statement, why the hell do I need to be told this? Of course I am going to be here, but Annie continues, "we will be sending another member of the team to physically remove John". Now I am really confused, "remove him", I state blankly, "I assume you mean collect him"? Annie's eyes dart to the others and back to me, which makes me feel uncomfortable. "No, I did mean remove him, we need him here, so we can get him rehabilitated as quickly as possible, so we can move forwards". I glance at Ms Rees, "who is going to remove him"? I instinctively ask, without even thinking. "We will be sending our CIA colleague, Mark, as he has been trained for these exact situations". Mark feels like an odd choice, baring in mind he has only just arrived at the team and he certainly doesn't know my John like I do. I am also confused about why anyone "physically" needs to go to remove John in the first place?

Annie receives a message on her phone, confirming the team haves successfully met with John and everything is now ready to go. As everyone files back in behind the glass, Mark enters the main room and walks towards me, a cocky strut of a walk, tucking a book inside his coat pocket as he approaches. From a side door a group of people enter the room, just as they did when my previous John arrived. "Don't worry Greg", Mark slyly sniggers at me, "I will take good care of John". I've hardly spent any time with Mark, but I already know I don't like him. I grit my teeth and smile as best as I can, trying to remain professional, "have a good trip, we can catch up when you get back", although I'd be happy if I never caught up with him again. Mark, just chuckles at me, "yeah when I'm back", is his strange and creepy reply! Annie quickly interjects, "come on you two, stop the gossiping, we have a job to do" and immediately takes Mark over to my spot, ready for him to go.

Twenty Five

I stand looking, well if I'm being honest, glaring, with evil dagger eyes at Mark. I realise I haven't seen the job being executed from this side before. I haven't seen a person disappear in front of me. I have seen my last John arrive so assume it will be similar. I feel slightly sick in my stomach, as I realise John will arrive shortly. I also realise that when John does arrive, he will be of a similar age to me, maybe this is why we've connected as we have.

Christian is ready to start and asks Mark if he is also ready? Mark nods back in his ugly confident manner. He is clearly unfazed by everything and just wants to get on with it. A klaxon suddenly sounds, making me jump, followed by a computer voice announcing a thirty second warning. Christian clearly wants to give Mark plenty of notice. As the countdown approaches ten seconds, my stomach cramps more with nerves. I recall reading about John being shot by some mad man, a crazy fan I think, which is just horrible. I don't really know any more than this but I hope he will arrive okay. Christian raises his hand to announce five seconds and starts the final countdown, four, three, two, one. Mark disappears instantly, no fading away, or flashing of lights, just one second there and the next, gone. After finishing his countdown, he confirms in his very next breath, "activated", while staring at me at the the whole time and clearly feeling uncomfortable. There follows another short pause, which feels like an eternity, before Christian announces, "here we go". There is a low brightness colour and John Lennon is suddenly standing right in front of me. It has worked and the whole process is just as incredible as last time, but holy shit, John Lennon is stood right there, in front of me, in 2019.

John looks visibly shocked and is holding himself, as if in pain. He quickly realises that he has transferred and he isn't in any pain at all. He is still trying to process the fact he hasn't died as he stands up tall, but struggling to speak. Then he shouts "Yeah", at the top of his voice. The word comes out of him sounding emotional and shaky. He doesn't shout anything else, just "Yeah". I instinctively call out to him, shaking with fear and move towards him quickly. John turns looking for me, trying to follow my voice, as we meet we grab hold of each other and both burst into tears. John is crying, floods of tears from the heartache and pain of losing his own life and maybe in relief that this worked. I am crying from the sheer emotion of it all and I am incredibly pleased and relieved to see him here. John's legs suddenly give way and we slump to the floor. I keep holding him until the tears subside, then as he starts to move slowly, he appears angry. "Why now"? he asks, which of course I can't answer. "I don't know I shrug, this is just how it was told in the history books. Some idiot fan apparently wanted to kill you, I don't know anymore than that, sorry". I hold onto him tightly, "Oh God", he cries over my shoulder, "poor Yoko and the boys". We sit on the floor until some men and women in white coats move in to collect John. They need to check him over and as this is a very stressful part of the repat process, they need to move quickly. I let go of John, "I will see you in a day or so". John nods at me and that is it, he is headed to the S.H. The people standing in the viewing area look shocked at what they have just witnessed and I feel like exhausted animal, sat on the floor of a zoo enclosure.

Christian is the first to approach me and he looks in shock as well. "I've never witnessed anything like that before", he manages to mutter, "holy shit are you okay"? I'm not really sure how I am, but I manage to confirm, "I'm okay". I pull myself together and stand up, starting to focus on the job again. Annie approaches me looking emotional, "what the heck was that", Annie asks, "that was one hell of an emotional reaction and you both have clearly bonded. Thank goodness you were here to greet him, or we would have had a major incident on our hands". Ms Rees also approaches, "well done Greg, you've proved today that you are one hundred percent the right person for the job. I'm literally still shaking", as she holds out her hands, as if to offer proof. We all congratulate ourselves on a job well done, "but where is Mark", I suddenly ask. "Mark? what do you mean"? challenges Annie. I look at them blankly, "Mark, you know, the guy you sent to remove John". Annie for the first time since I've known her, looks lost for words. Ms Rees steps in, "Mark won't be returning to us for a while, he is being detained you see. At some point in the near future Annie will get him released and send him off to do another job, but right now, he's not coming back". I glance at everyone in the group quickly, "Why"? which I think is a reasonable question, aimed at Ms Rees. "That's because he was the person that killed John Lennon and he was arrested at the scene". I'm suddenly confused and a weird pain pulses through me, like I was the one that had been shot. "Hang on a minute, are you telling me that we were the ones who killed John Lennon"? My brain, feels like it's shutting down, likes it's about to explode, "if you hadn't sent Mark, whatever his name is, today, then John would still be alive and could have lived to an old age"? I'm so confused, I read about his death years ago, so history has already been written, yet it hadn't really been written, because we wrote history today? What the hell is happening? I am angry, shocked and disappointed to learn that because of our actions, John Lennon has died at the age of 40, back in 1980, which was only a few minutes ago in this very room. The room feels like it is spinning, as I try to grasp a hold of any sort of reality. If we hadn't done what we had, would John Lennon have lived to become an old man? My brain is about to explode? Have we really changed the course of history? I glare at the others in the room, "why? why did we kill John Lennon at such a young age"? Ms Rees, without a single look of emotion, replies, "because we need him here right now, to help us make many millions in revenues, which keeps you and everyone in work. It also means we can then have enough funding to go on with this project and save many more people from history! It was a necessary evil I'm afraid and you did a perfect job today in saving our future generations".

I need to get out of here, so I quickly shower and change, leaving exhausted and mentally drained. It is now early in the afternoon and the rain has stopped. I practically fall into my car, knowing I need to get myself home. As I drive down the long driveway, The Beatles songs connect to the music system in the car. My mood couldn't be any further away from the one I felt this morning, so I quickly turn the sound all the way down. I've had some tough days in my life, but none have come even close to today. I need to go home to see my family and drink some beers.

Twenty Six

I pull up onto my driveway and know I must put on
a brave face before I walk in the door. The twins
wouldn't care if I'd had a bad day at work, let
alone understand that technically, I think, I may
have been involved in the murder of John Lennon.
Bonnie has always told me to leave my work on
the driveway! Work late if you have to, but the
moment you walk through the door, work is
finished and family time starts. I have forgotten the
number of times I have sat in the car finishing off
phone calls, so I can give one hundred percent
attention when I do walk in. This is absolutely the

right thing to do, as the twins are only young once. They aren't interested in my day, good or bad, they just want to tell me about theirs. So today, more than any other day, I will leave my job on the driveway. I breath out heavily, shake my head, like I am warming up for a boxing match and open the front door. I am welcomed by the glorious noise of the twins arguing and Bonnie shouting at them to sit down and eat their food. I have never been happier to hear the chaos that enveloped me at that very moment. Bonnie flashes a smile in my direction, followed by, "how was your day"? Which is unheard of, my response is, "oh you know, boring really, with lots of spreadsheets". The twins are finally sat down and eating, as I ask them about their day. They both answer at the same time as usual and I don't really understand what they are going on about, as usual, but it doesn't matter, as it just makes me feel warm inside. Bonnie wanders over and gives me a hug from the back of the chair, which again is unheard of and I even hear her whisper softly in my ear, "you look tired, I will take the kids to their swimming clubs tonight, so you can have a break". It is one of the best things I have heard in a long time and of course I accept immediately. With the kids and Bonnie out of the house I drink a few beers, hit the shower again, as I still feel dirty from the day. Falling into bed, I am fast asleep before they all arrive back home again. I vaguely remember Bonnie sliding into bed next to me, trying to snuggle and possibly play, I bizarrely say, "sorry not tonight". This is clearly not my finest move, but today has been exceptionally strange and I feel justified, although Bonnie is clearly put out.

I wake late the next morning and the house is empty, as everyone has already left for school and a shopping trip, as confirmed by the lovely little note on the fridge. Deep down I know I need to go into work today, not for anyone else, but for my own sanity. The drive passes quickly as my mind is racing over the previous days events and as I arrive, Christian is also just heading into the building. "Morning", I shout over to him, to get his attention before we go in. "Morning shithead", is his predictable yet joyful reply. As I catch up with him, I ask, "what the hell was that all about yesterday"? Christian in fairness appears to be as lost as me, but does confirm, "I honestly didn't know anything about it all". I never doubted this and he continues, "I went home last night and searched the internet for hours, looking for anything and everything on John Lennon, on his life and more importantly, his death and it all stacks up. Did we change history? Who knows? It appears it's always been written that way, so we have to assume this is how it always was, we were just there at the right time to save him, thankfully. Interestingly that little prick, Mark Chapman, shot him in his back and rather than run from the murder scene, he just sat down and read him a few chapters from a book called, The Catcher In The

Rye, what the hell is that all about? The internet also states he is still locked up for the murder, even after all these years! Of course that's assuming he's actually still there and assuming he even went to prison in the first place"? I can't believe my ears, but feel a little comforted that history had already been written, before we were involved - I think?

We both walk into the building, ready for whatever is thrown at us today. Annie is already waiting, "Good morning you lazy pair, how are you feeling today"? My response is an open and honest, "I'm very tired, mentally exhausted and confused, but I want to see if I can meet up with John today, to see how he is settling in, if that's okay"? Annie, back to her brilliant best, "I knew that's what you would want so I've already sent the request through, the reply is positive, but you've been asked to keep the visit short as John recovers from this stressful transition". This is music to my ears, "absolutely" is my firm, but happy reply, "I don't want to stress him out, I just want to make sure he's fine, when can I go to him"? Annie smiling back, like she is giving me a birthday present, "right now if you want to"? Annie genuinely looks pleased to authorise it, "Christian will you show Greg the way down to sub-level 4 please".

As we leave the room and enter the lift to go down four floors, Christian in a warm friendly voice says, "good luck, I hope it goes well, but come and find me for a chat afterwards if you need to" and it feels like he genuinely means it. As the doors open Christian point me towards a desk, where a nurse is stood behind. I turn, just in time to see the doors closing and Christian heading back upstairs, as I'm left with no one to hold my metaphorical hand. As I approach the desk, the nurse stands and pleasantly greets me, "good morning, we've been expecting you, please follow me". I feel quite strange, although I realise a lot of my feelings since I have started this job have been new and strange to me. Pushing open the door to John's room and there, sat up in bed in front of me, is my friend and I am relieved to see he has a huge smile on his face. I blurt out, "Oh man are you okay"? to which John confirms, "yeah all good, but I could do with a decent cuppa, the stuff in here is like dishwater". The tension is broken instantly, "how are you really though"? John winces a little, "well I wasn't expecting to be here so soon, if I'm being honest with you and I feel like Yoko, Sean and Julian have died and not the other way around. But look man, I'm okay, I knew this day would come and I was ready for it. Over the last few years I've found peace and I have accepted my destiny, knowing that when the time came it was to seek a higher purpose, to make a difference, you know? As a result I have lived my life a certain way and fought hard for various things, having the perspective of life after death, if you want to call it that. Look this isn't going to be easy, but I'm ready for the next chapter of my life, err, well death I suppose. I met a lovely doctor this morning and she has been telling me the names of others that have arrived here before me and man I'm excited to collaborate with them". John pulls a note book from his side table, "look I've even got a new note book to start me off". John opens the first page and there are a list of names written down. John glances at me, "although", he continues, "I've not heard of some of the people that have arrived before me, like Amy Winehouse? or a George Michael? I'm told they are awesome so I guess I need to get up to speed with these people quickly and the new sounds". I smile warmly, "I am so pleased for you John, you can't change the past, history is history, but you can go on to live an amazing future and help us to make the World a better place". After a few minutes talking with John he is starting to look tired, "I guess this dying thing takes it out of you", I say, "so I'm gonna get out of your hair and we can catch up again soon, yeah"? John enthusiastically confirms, "of course we can Greg, I'm going to be here from now on, I mean in the here and now, so we can hang out a lot more. None of this setting a date for the 9th of February in some future year and hoping you will turn up". It is amazing to think I can see him more often, "cool", is my response, as I start to head for the door. John calls me back though, "listen Greg, I found out something truly amazing this morning. A few years ago I told Paul about us pair always meeting up on the 9th February, I obviously didn't tell him everything" he laughs, "it may seem a bit crazy I guess, but the number 9 and more importantly the 9th, has always been a special date to me. I did so many amazing things on that very day, all because of our relationship. So you have literally made history with me, which is cool. I even made Paul promise, that if I die and he has a big deal thing going on in his life, that he would do it on the 9th of February, you know, as a way of remembering me. So this morning, the nice doctor I was telling you about, did a search on something called the internet. Now that's a great invention, literally everything in the World in one place. Anyway, she search up Paul, to see what he's been up to since I left in 1980 and guess what"? John has me listening intently, "go on I say eagerly". "Well, Paul made the 9th February 1993, as the date to release his solo album, which is a nice touch and I would have been happy with that, but wait, there's more. Paul also agreed to receive a star on the Hollywood Walk Of Fame, as long as it was on, you guessed it, the 9th February, this time in 2012. How friggin awesome is that"? John has a real glint in his eye, as he thinks of Paul honouring him, years after his death! "That is so exciting, it must be great to look back at the last 50 years to catch up on everything, in one single morning". John has clearly loved searching the internet for his family and the group, "Yeah it was pretty sweet", he says smiling back, "did you know that I even have my own Hollywood Walk Of Fame Star now? I made it, just like Elvis"! Without thinking, I correct him to "Aron", which shows I have finally settled in here.

I am genuinely pleased for John and I am relieved to see he is happy and as settled as he can be right now, "I need to go John, or I will be moaned at soon, but I am so pleased you are here and I can see lots more of you. Try and take it easy for a few days, then you'll find yourself busier than ever writing music and songs, for the likes of Ed Sheeran". John looks a little confused, "I suppose that's another person I need to look up on the internet thing"? I realise how strange this must all be for John, "let's catch up soon, as long as you can fit me into your new busy life", I suggest. John makes the peace sign at me, which is instantly one of the most exciting moments in my life, I am actually seeing living history being displayed in front of me, that is, until he turns his hand around and laughs, "now piss off". I shake my head playfully, as I leave the room, this iconic man is just perfect and he's provided me with the inner peace I need today.

Twenty Seven

As I stroll around the gardens trying to clear my head and gather my thoughts, I receive a text from Annie, asking me to meet in her office to discuss my next John. I like the fact that my targets are no longer referred to as targets, but now "John's". It is certainly a fitting tribute to my first two cases. I still feel tired, but I am intrigued to find out who my next John will be. I head straight to Annie's office and remind myself how incredibly lucky I am to work in a place like this, despite the tough last few days. I knock on Annie's door and enter by leaning around the door at the same time, as I feel slightly awkward about just walking in without Annie's confirmation. "Oh come on in Greg", Annie announces, as friendly as ever. "How are you feeling now"? "I'm okay", I reply, sounding a little shaky, "it's been a hard few days I guess, with plenty to think about, but I'm okay". Annie leads me to her amazing sofa and continues, "we want you to be happy here and you've certainly settled in extremely well. We know how tough this job can be and I'm sorry I couldn't share the full information with you about Mark and the outcome. I realise now that this was a mistake and I'm sorry for that. Christian has brought me right up to speed about the work you've done, how we can fully trust you and in the future I will make sure you are included in all aspects of your case. We all make mistakes from time to time, but I suppose the key thing is to admit when we are wrong and to learn from our mistakes. I am keen for this team to be together for many years, with you leading it, based on your experiences, especially those from recent times. I guess you would have learned a lot and how to apply those things in the future? Look, we aren't saying we are perfect, but I am keen to avoid a blame culture, so if anything is wrong, we need to talk about it, my door is always open for you. We can discuss, analyse and make corrections, so we can hopefully, avoid doing the same things again. Agreed"? Annie offers me her immaculately clean and finger nail polished hand. I grasp her hand, conscious of not overly squeezing it, but aware I don't want to appear weak either and nod, while stating a firm, "agreed", back to Annie. "Good, now let's clean the slate and move on to the next job shall we. Are you ready to start right back at the beginning"? I confirm, "I am definitely ready, but I will need a few days off to get over everything. The last few days have exhausted me, both physically and mentally. I need to take some time off and come back fresh for my next challenge". Annie, leans back into the sofa and smirks, "I'm very impressed Greg, you know you need to be ready, or you won't be giving one hundred percent to the job and I like that! I said from the outset that you could take as much time off as you wanted and these are the exact reasons for that. Why don't you fly your family to my private island for the week, you can have access to my private jet and pilot, as I'm not going anywhere this week. There's everything there that you are going to need, for a great family break. What do you say"? I am yet again, blown away by Annie, who continues to be a few steps ahead of me and I can't say anything, other than, "that would be amazing, thank you, as long as you're sure of course"? Annie frowns at me in a playful, non bossy way, "I wouldn't have offered, if I wasn't sure, would I? Now head home and pack your bags, enjoy yourselves and then come back fighting fit".

As I say my goodbyes and far too many thank you's, I am instantly excited, who could resist an expensive sunny holiday, on a private island, with a private jet? I know I can't and surely Bonnie will be in agreement. Holidays are about getting off the fast spinning World for a while and spending quality time with your family. I practically skip to the car, the tired, lethargic feeling has mysteriously disappeared from my body. I start the engine and switch on the music, which still has The Beatles playing on the system. How did I drive to work today not hearing the music playing? I was clearly distracted by the recent events. I quickly switch off The Beatles, weirdly glancing to the sky to say "sorry John", like he is dead, to play The Beach Boys, as these tunes have holiday, written all over them. I calmly drive down the sweeping driveway, although I desperately want to plant my foot to the floor and scream all the way along it.

As I join the main road I call Bonnie, "hey how's things"? I start all calm like it is just another normal phone call. "Yeah I'm all good", is her reply, "I'm a little lost and bored if I'm being honest though", she sighs. "Well, how do you fancy getting away for a bit"? Bonnie replies very quickly "what yes, oh hang on we've got the twins school and clubs to think about", I sigh heavily, deliberately heavy, "Bonnie listen, we all need a break and the twins missing a few days of school and clubs won't matter, they'll have a much better time where we will be going". I feel very manly in my response, as I hear "Hmmmm, I'm not sure", Bonnie is clearly not sold on the idea, "where do you have in mind"? "Well"... I pause, trying to build a bit of tension, "just a private jet to my bosses private island, that's all". Bonnie screams with excitement, which I've not heard her do for several years and this makes me excited as well. My speech suddenly quickens, "listen Bonnie, I'm on my way home right now, so go and pick up the twins from school, then start packing as soon as you get home, because we are leaving tomorrow morning". Bonnie seems genuinely happy and that's before she can share the news with the twins, who will both be completely blown away with the surprise. I finish the call and ring Annie, "I just want to say thank you again for the use of your island, I've spoken with Bonnie and she is over the moon". Annie chuckles down the phone, "I'm just really pleased its all worked out for you, you deserve a break and we will definitely get more out of you when your back so don't worry, it's a win, win. By the way", she continues, "I didn't tell you about your next John, did I". "Oh my God you're right", I suddenly feel a mixture of being horrified and embarrassed, "I'm so sorry, I was too wrapped up in my own life". Annie clearly doesn't mind, "honestly it's not a problem and in fairness we will need the next few days, to get this one all mapped out, it's not going to be easy at all". I am desperate to find out more, "so who's my next John", I eagerly ask? Annie, cheekily asks if I am sitting down, deliberately playing with me, before launching into, "Greg, your next John, or should I say our, next John is the scientist Rosalind Franklin".

Twenty Eight

I am aware I'm waking up in a different bed, my
head hurts and my brain is clouded, as I try to
figure out where I am, or more importantly when?
It is still early in the day, well early for me anyway,
as I sit up and rub my hair, trying to focus. After all
this travelling between different years, you'd think
I'd be used to all this now. I remember leaving for
this trip slightly early, just so I could get away
from home, as I see a yellow folder on the side
board. It was there on my arrival yesterday, but if
I'm being honest I decided to ignore it until today,
as I just needed some me time. I slowly piece it all

together in my mind. Last night did just the trick, after I arrived early to enjoy a night of peace, no hassle, no stress, just me and a bed.

I shuffle slowly towards the folder and catch sight of myself in the mirror, a tired looking and unattractive image looking back at me. Gone are the days where I can jump out of bed, instantly ready to tackle the day. I fold back the yellow front cover and I'm presented with a photo of a man, mid forties, not unattractive, looking back at me. He looks like someones brother, or a regular person living next door to you. This is to be my target and one that as usual, I need to ensure says yes, a no just won't suit my boss. My boss that I've learned over time, never accepts a no for an answer.

The target's name is Greg Oban, who is an atypical family man, with a wife and two children, twins by all account. The year I have been sent back to is 2019 and I know we don't have too long to get my target signed up to the program, trained and tested, before the job of all jobs is presented to him. If I fail, there is no point in my returning back to 2102 and there will be no point in hiding, as I would be caught and of course erased. I need to make this work and a meeting in a coffee shop is just what I need this morning to wake me up.

As I arrive I instantly recognise my target, who is sitting at the rear of the coffee shop. He appears to be looking around and clearly comfortable in this environment. I need to be on my A game today, I need to be forceful, but remain ladylike. There is no point in flirting with Greg, as this had been tried and tested during the past few months by the team based here. Each time someone has met with Greg and flirted, he either doesn't know he is being flirted with, or he is just not interested, confirming his allegiance to his wife and family. I read he is incredibly loyal, despite being baited and he has proved to be a worthy candidate. I am determined to challenge this finding, but today is not the day to start this, today is purely about getting Greg's attention and getting results.

I casually walk straight towards Greg in my business outfit, deliberately chosen to fit in with this part of town and era. I walk straight up to my target and say "hi, you must be Greg, we spoke on the phone". Greg is slightly confused at how I recognise him, but as I have been informed in the brief, I shouldn't be challenged. Greg looks more handsome in the flesh, the picture not really doing him much justice. Business men usually try and control the meeting from the beginning, but this is not a game I like to play. I like to be in charge and if I am being honest, I need to be in charge, after all, as my father used to tell me, there is only one Annie in this World, so go out there and be the best you, that you can be.

As much as I want to get straight to the point of why I am here, I am all too much aware that certain protocols dictate a slightly slower pace to a meeting here in 2019. Greg, after all believes he is here to sell me his products, when in reality, we have set up this meeting to sell Tx3 to him. Ms Rees and her team have studied hundreds of people over the past year, eventually whittling it down to a handful of candidates, but as the history books will show, there is really only one person who will be offered this role of a lifetime. A role that we all hope will save the lives of millions of people. So as much as this goes against my every fibre of my being, I know I have to open with the weather and the news events that I have read about in the file. I have read so many documents on my target, that I know him and his lifestyle incredibly well. After the boring, but apparently essential weather chat, I need to get things moving, "I appreciate you meeting me this morning. Also meeting me first thing, as I'm sure you'd have preferred to go into the office straight after the school run and meet later in the day, but this time works better for me today. Time, you see Greg, is a strange thing. We all think we have lots of it when we are young, we feel we will live forever and then all of a sudden we are in our mid forties and we start worrying that we are running out of time". I am doing my best to appear seductive, without being overly flirtatious and I want to appear mysterious at this stage of the meeting. I knew from a young age that I was put on this planet to achieve something big and this could be the beginning of it all.

While I have his attention I continue, "my business is time". Leaning forwards, just like I have been taught in my training, "most people think they want flash cars, or expensive houses, but the truly rich want more time, more time with their family, more time to do the jobs around the house that they can't do, because they are working all the time. Time for holidays, time for experiences, time for themselves to go play sport with a friend, time to be alone with their wife and not have to worry about the kids... time my friend is the most valuable thing in the world right now. Time is what we all need more of and time, if used wisely, can change everything". I sit back, very pleased with myself and take a sip of my tea, it's like I am on the stage performing. All the previous jobs I've had, have led me to this moment. Greg babbles something back, about it only being that simple and making excuses, I decide to cut him off with, "you are absolutely right, but my business is all about time and I want you to come onboard to ensure we are using our time wisely. Look... you can stay in your job until you retire, you can keep trying to hit the targets, even though they increase them every year. You can pay the bills, keep the kids in their school clubs and their video games, hell..... you can even play Squash occasionally but you know deep down, you, need, more. You need the old you back, the happy person you've lost along the way, the stress free you. Now let's just say I can offer you all that and you get more free time than you can ever remember and you only come to work when you've had enough holidaying, when you are looking for the next challenge - when you are really ready to work. More money than you can think about, but most importantly, with this offer comes the time you crave! What do you say? Why not come and work for us, at Tx3"?

I can sense Greg is hooked, I can just see it in his eyes. He is a nice man, who has succeeded in his job and despite working long hours, he still manages to find time for his family. But time has taken its toll on him. He is still fairly young and ambitious, not to climb the corporate ladder, but for the lifestyle he so desperately craves. I know at this point I need to be quiet, to watch him squirm and to see if he can analyse the situation knowing he has to process it all quickly. Greg responds about being intrigued, but wanting to know more. I am relieved, it has worked, it has gone to plan and to use a sporting term I am out of the starting blocks. "Trust me, after I show you our business you won't be able to say no". I am amused at how Greg's head is clearly spinning but he confirms, "well in that case Annie, I'm free for a few hours next week, so why don't I take you up on that challenge and see what happens". This is my opportunity to leave him with the hook, the part of any good meeting that you remember above any other part, so smiling my best rehearsed smile, I whisper part A of that hook, "that's not a challenge, it's a promise, a promise that your time will not be wasted in the slightest". Greg confirms we can meet next week, so I am able to finish the meeting with part B of the hook, "Greg why don't you just head home for the day, pretend this meeting went on longer than anticipated, after all, you will be handing in your notice soon anyway"! Damn I'm good, I smirk as I leave Greg there and head back to my apartment, which is not too far away.

I could return to base at this point I suppose, but after the last few days at home, I decide to stay here and enjoy some much needed time for myself. Things haven't been easy for a long time, but the abuse over the last few months have increased to a much higher level. In the past I fought back, but recently I've just accepted the punches, given the impression of submission. This of course is not in my DNA and I have a long term plan hatching, in order to resolve this situation. Today however, is a good day, a day that has gone to plan and I can relax now and enjoy the peacefulness.

Greg's email arrives on the Thursday, after what is clearly a waiting game. I confirm the meeting and agree to send a car to pick him up, at ten on Monday morning. This I believe is a beautiful sweetener and will instantly engage his brain with what is coming. All is now set, I just need to go into Tx3, to meet the team and the boss of this operation in person. I need to make sure everything continues to go smoothly, as I can't afford for this to go wrong now.

Twenty Nine

I feel the most relaxed I have felt in a long time. It's nice to not have any of the stress I've been getting at home recently, from my overpowering husband, just me, in my own skin. As I arrive at Tx3 for my first meeting, I am welcomed by a strange English man, "good morning ma'am". What a strange, old fashioned way to meet people, it must give a sense of grandeur. As I enter the amazing glass building, I am incredibly impressed with the size. Although in fairness this may appear to be expensive for this era, but money is much more valuable in the future, we then distribute it to the past. I'm aware that its true cost equivalent is only a few thousand pounds of our future money. So whilst this is one impressive building, of the here and now, I know it's not really that expensive.

I can see Ms Rees approaching, who looks just like her photo that I'd been shown in the debrief. I am also fully aware of how dangerous this lady can be and I am determined to get off on the right footing. Her great, great granddaughter, is my boss back at base and between them, they have no morals at all and I can quite easily be wiped out.

"Hi, lovely to meet you", is my opening line, quickly followed by, "this is a great set up you have here". Ms Rees half smiles, before stating firmly, "we all know what this really cost the company, so let's not over do the niceties". That certainly put me in my place and concerns me, as we have Greg arriving on Monday and we need to impress him enough to sign up on the day and Ms

Rees is not exactly the picture of warmth. "Follow me, I need to show you my office, which will become your office. After that I will introduce you to the team, as our new head of Tx3", Ms Rees announces, clearly in control here. As we enter her office, Ms Rees is quick to close the door behind me so we can talk freely, "I have told everyone that I am moving to CEO, so you effectively become the head around here. We are the only two people that know what is really happening at this point, to avoid any complications". This of course makes perfect sense and I am ready to get stuck in. "Greg will arrive here on Monday", I announce like Ms Rees isn't aware, but of course I am swiftly reminded who the boss is and that she knows about everything going on here.

We decide it will make sense to meet the team, so they are familiar with me and Greg will not suspect anything. The first on this list will be a man called Christian, who I am told will be key to Greg and the team. Christian has practically built the time traveller, believing himself to be a genius. What Christian is not aware of, is that all the parts and ideas have been cleverly planted and fed to him, from the future, based on a unit that we have been using successfully for several years. Christian is essentially an operator, make no mistake, he is a brilliant operator all the same, carrying out an incredibly difficult role. "He is extremely loyal, happy and believes everything we tell him. His relationship with Greg will be key, if we run into any difficulties".

Following a whistle stop tour and a meeting with everyone to introduce myself, I am ready for a Greg's arrival on Monday. In my mind we are done, I understand the brief, the layout of the areas within this building that I need to know and I have been given the necessary equipment, phone, laptop etc. Ms Rees however has other ideas, "we have already successfully captured several people from the past to help us with our journey", she starts, "the repat injection was a huge turning point for us, we had already been using the boomerang technique and serum, from our post generations, but boy did the discovery of the repat change our program". I'd never really thought much about the technology involved with this program, it has been around for such a long time and well before I was involved. "So how did the repat serum help the program in this time"? I enquire, Ms Rees is clearly in her element with this question, especially as I am genuinely interested and not just asking for the sake of it. "Let's walk and talk", she states, as she heads off down a corridor towards the lifts. "Let's head down to sub-level 8", she proudly announces, while swiping her security clearance. I wasn't even aware that the levels went down that far. As we enter the lift Ms Rees continues, "when we started this program here, we could only capture people and bring them back, in the hopes they would agree to work for us. Also, depending on the age and health of the person, we might only keep them for a year or so before they died, which was very inconvenient, after all the time and energy we had put into them. Then our post generation colleagues were able to make the repat serum work, so they quickly brought this to us here about five years ago and it has literally transformed our operation to what it is today. Now whoever we repat, are not only incredibly fit and healthy, but they never age beyond the age of arrival, never. The icing on the cake though was the discovery in the second iteration where a slight tweak ensured they arrive as the most loyal subjects you can ever have". I am aware that the program could repat people, but I wasn't aware of the full details, so this is news to me. "Are you saying that everyone here is completely in the company's control and working hard for the cause"? Ms Rees is clearly enjoying this moment, as the doors of the lift open. We step out onto a mezzanine floor, overlooking a vast room, which is easily the biggest room I have ever seen. Below us and within this huge space are hundreds of pods, with a small gap between them, probably about a metre between each of them. "Every pod is identical", Ms Rees confirms, "they are all three and a half metres square, which is the perfect size for a bed, a shower and a small table and chair. These people don't need, or indeed want anything else and they have time to read, or simply relax. The program allows them to head to their designated areas to work on their chosen field, during the times we allow them to of course, for the rest of the time they are here. Never wanting for anything, as we provide the food, water, heating and clothes, which means they can give one hundred percent capacity to the tasks being asked of them". We continue down the stairs and arrive at bay one, "This bay is for the entertainers, whether it be actors, singers or musicians, you get my drift. They have been the backbone to this operation, sometimes teaching the newer generations, but mainly just here to entertain our employees. The singers often teach the younger generations, they continue to write music and songs, which we in turn sell, so we can make money to feed these poor souls and fund ourselves of course. We learned a while back, that we can't keep requesting funds from our post generations, as they are clearly expecting us to fund ourselves".

"Bay two is for the political figures, these generally have an incredible brain capacity to process information and problem solve for us. Where they have been invaluable, is providing the security details in various countries, which has in turn allowed us to recruit even more successfully. There is one political leader I would like you to meet as he will assist your meeting on Monday, that is the illustrious John F Kennedy". We slowly pass the first pod, labelled Mrs Margaret Thatcher, who is sat at her desk writing. The second pod was labelled as indicated Mr John F Kennedy and he too is at his desk writing. Ms Rees taps the glass window and he immediately looks up at us. From what I have seen and heard so far, I expected a robot like response, but I couldn't have been any further from the truth. Mr Kennedy, appears normal and very friendly as he approaches the front of the pod. Ms Rees presses another button and the glass disappears, as Mr Kennedy offers me his hand to shake, looking exactly as he did in the photos I have seen of him. "Good morning", he says politely, "how can I assist you"? Ms Rees replies, "This is Annie St Hillier who will be heading up Tx3 for a while and on Monday we have a new recruit coming here, to be shown around and encouraged to join us. If we call for you on Monday, would you be kind enough to show your face to our new recruit, as we feel this will make all the difference to the process"? John is as charming as you'd expect him to be, "why, yes of course I can, just call when you are ready for me and I will be waiting, I would be delighted to help". "Thank you John", is all Ms Rees says, before pressing the button again and John returns to his writing desk, which is very surreal.

As we turn to head back in the direction we came, Ms Rees continues, "there are clearly lots of others here at our disposal, but if we are to succeed we require the services of some key figures, which of course is where Greg comes into this. Money is not flowing into our business like it did previously, some of the artists are simply out of date and out of touch and very shortly we will make a decision on who we need to retain and who has become surplus to requirements. Those who are not paying their way, need to be terminated. We need to get Greg up to speed quickly, so we can then turn his efforts to finding the right people to resolve the minor, so called global pandemic, of COVID-19. Not because we need to solve that issue, as we all know a vaccine will be found, but the people we put in place this time, urgently need to continue with their research, or the true global pandemic of 2103, will literally kill hundreds of millions of people and potentially wipe out the human race altogether. No pressure then Annie"!

Ms Rees accompanies me back through the building, reminding me of the key areas ahead of my meeting with Greg. As I leave the building, my head hurts and the pressure has certainly increased beyond anything I have known previously.

Thirty

Monday morning arrives quickly and despite my best efforts to relax over the weekend, it has been challenging. If anything, I am just relieved to be getting on with the day, so I arrive at Tx3 early, settle into my office to get ready to receive Greg. I have a quick meeting with Ms Rees, who confirms all is set. I sit at my PC screen and nervously follow the tracker on the car, that we sent to collect him. The clock reads eleven thirteen and as they approach, the electric gates are opened, ready for their arrival. The car turns off the main road and onto the sweeping driveway, without stopping.

Greg is welcomed into the building and I walk to meet him, smiling and holding out my hand. I am determined to relax him immediately, so as I shake his hand I gesture a kiss, which he does, just as we say "hi". I immediately follow with, "Greg I want you to relax, feel comfortable and ask as many questions you want, after all today is not a job interview, as I'm sure you would have thought of it in that way. In simple terms we want you, so the role is yours if you want it. My job today is to show you enough of what we do, how we do it and of course where you fit into all this. We have spent the last few months researching you, your family and your lifestyle to know we have the right person for this role, I only ask that you keep an open mind please". I direct us to the office, at the rear of the building, making sure to head straight there. Once inside I direct Greg to Ms Rees' sofa or my sofa as it will be known. "Do you think you could get to like it here? In fairness you wouldn't be here very often, but when you do need to visit I want you to feel proud of where you work". I continue, "during our walk around I will show you a few spaces where I think your office can be and you can let me know which one you'd prefer. For now though, let me tell you a little about this company, what we are trying to achieve and the role we know you are perfect for. Once we have finished, I can give you a demonstration to really bring it all to life." Wow, I feel like I am on fire, fully in control and if I'm being honest I am enjoying myself, which is the first time in a long time, that I can say that.

"Finally, I have been a little presumptuous sorry", I elaborate, "I have asked for your company car to be brought here today. Assuming you are happy to join us, then you might as well drive yourself home tonight. After all of this, to pre-warn you, I will be asking you how you feel, if you're in, or out? I will be looking for some sort of commitment and yes I appreciate you may want to discuss this at home, but I would appreciate your feedback at that point". I can sense Greg is lapping it all up and his eyes are definitely widening with anticipation, I am convinced I've already caught my fish.

I take Greg on a tour of the building and I am genuinely excited to show off the technology that is clearly light years ahead of the rest of this time period. However, I can't really get into a huge amount of detail, as I only arrived a few days ago myself, so I'm not exactly up to full speed yet. It would be a disaster if I tell him about technology from the future and mess up this whole operation. So my plan is to keep everything at a high level and I'm sure it's working. With the guided tour complete we are approached by a smart young man, bringing me the keys to Greg's new car, which I am confident will impress him. I am about to thank the young man, but realise I don't know his name, or even his position in this company. Instead I move us out to the car and I am genuinely blown away by its beauty. Cars where I'm from are boring, functional dual cell, hydro powered, square boxes that pilot themselves. As a child growing up I would often read about the old days and how cars were actually driven by people and the noise, smell and power were apparently incredible. So to actually see this beautiful looking car, in all its shining glory is truly a moment to savour. Greg is about to get in the wrong side, which amuses me, as even I know what side you need to sit in to drive and I'm not even from here. I quickly ask Greg, "why are you going to the passenger side? how on earth are you going to drive it if you sit that side"?

Greg strangely returns my question with his own "why would you want me to drive your car? Surely you will want to take her for a spin before anyone else does"? It is at this point I realise Greg thinks the car is mine, "Greg, I don't think you realise what is happening here? this is your car, the car I was telling you about earlier, the one I thought you might like to drive home tonight".

The young man standing next to me, chips in with, "the key Sir, you have the key in the box", as he is also running out of patience and rolling his eyes at me. I push Greg a little further, "take the car for spin to see what you think". Greg appears more than happy to oblige as he enters the car, starts her up and drives away.

As Greg leaves us standing here, the young man next to me, immediately directs me back into the building. "Ma'am we need to move quickly, my instructions from Ms Rees, are t0 call for JFK at this precise moment, so we can keep this meeting on track". He is right of course and we quickly walk back inside. I authorise the request and also ask the security team to track Greg in the car, so we know exactly where he is and more importantly, when he's returning. The building suddenly comes alive with people rushing to get everything set up, which is the complete opposite to what I've experienced to date. JFK arrives a few minutes later and agrees to wait in another room. A few minutes later again, I receive the call to confirm Greg is returning. I walk back to meet him as he arrives and chat to him as we return to my office once more. I need to capture the moment, as Greg has clearly loved the car, so I need to keep up his interest with, "a few bullet points to whet your appetite and to demonstrate how serious we are, in hiring you. Firstly the wage, I know money is important to you but I also know that it's not all about money. Yes I know you want to support your family and make them as secure as possible, but you also want time to spend with them. Gone are the days where you get to go home and put up your feet in the evening. There is always one club or another that you need to get to, right? And you sometimes skip off work early to ensure you get there on time. I also know that once the twins are in bed, you often open up your laptop and start work again, just so you can fit it all in, so, let's get the wages part out of the way : we will pay you four million pounds a year for this role and I'm hoping this will take the pressure off you and your wife and life can become more.... well, manageable again".

It worked, I've certainly caught his attention and he is like a small boy, in the palm of my hand. "Secondly, as I've said before, you would be able to take as much time off work as you need and when you're ready you can report in for duty. What I want, is for you to want to work, to want to be here and want to help in changing the lives of millions of people. You can only do this if you are fully committed and ready, therefore you must holiday as much as you need to, so you can achieve this. This could be weeks or even months at a time".

To use a boxing analogy, I have him on the ropes and I just need to keep the punches coming, but I am keen to get some buy in from Greg. "The perks like healthcare etc we can get into another day, but can we agree that this is a great way to start"? Greg's reply is a little vague, "the terms seems generous", is what he actually says, however he does then follow this with, "I am slightly concerned about what I am expected to do, in order to receive this package". There it is, the hook. I now know that I have peaked enough interest in him, but I need to give him something more concrete or risk losing the opportunity. I need to deliver the final blow. I quickly hit send on my phone, with my message to call for Mr Kennedy, for his big moment. I then continue, "Greg, whilst I would like to tell you everything about your role, I simply cannot, that is until you accept the position. What I can say is that all of us here at Tx3 are very happy with our choice in you. We know you are exactly the right person for the job and the way you have handled today has only reaffirmed this. I think it will help to give you a little demonstration now, as promised, which will hopefully show you what we are all about. The role we want you to do is simple, we just want you to talk to the people we ask you to, about time and Tx3. In reality the job is pretty similar to what you do now, you meet people, get to know them and talk to them about the product, the offering if you like. The people you meet however, will not be easy to convince, but lives depend on you getting them to understand the benefits of joining up with us here at Tx3. Sounds straightforward right? But every time we send you off to meet someone, we are very keen for you to get the deal done. We cannot accept no for an answer, so it could mean you having to make several trips and that is why we are prepared to pay you handsomely. While you stay with your family we are happy for you to be with them, but when you are with us, we need you to be one hundred percent focused on getting the job done. This could take years in some cases but you must stick with the job until it is complete. Now I appreciate that sounds like a huge payoff... this could involve you

being away from your young family for a few
weeks or even months at a time, however each
time you return we make sure, that in reality you
have only been away for a few seconds. So from
the outside it would look like you've come here to
your office, in your new company car and then go
home again on the same day. To reassure you this
is even possible and that we have all the time we
want on our hands, please let me demonstrate.
Greg, please welcome a very important person in
this company, he is our President, in fact he is THE
President. Greg, please say hello to President John
F Kennedy"!

I am so relieved that the plan has worked and come
together perfectly. Greg is clearly as confused as
I'd hoped he would be. He mutters something
under his breath as JFK, calmly walks towards
him, smiling and holding out his hand to greet him.
"Hi Greg, it's a pleasure to meet you. This must be
a strange day for you? Let me just say, I'm am

forever indebted to Tx3 and I will never regret making time to speak with them, it turned out to be invaluable! I will leave you finalise your contract with Annie and we can catch up the next time our paths cross. Welcome to your amazing new life in Tx3, the amazing people you will meet, plus the wonderful places this job will no doubt take you to". And with that, he obediently turns and leaves the room, he is superb and as brilliant as Ms Rees confirmed he would be. I decide to finish with, "I think that concludes my demonstration. What do you think"? Greg appears to be impressed, so I finish the day with more details about his role before confirming he will work with only one target at a time. What I really want to move onto is the whole concept of time travel, so I remind him, "Sometimes you can be away for a day or a week and on the rare occasion, months. However, you can return at any point to Tx3, in the knowledge that you have in reality only been away for a few seconds".

I don't really want to dwell on this part too long and quickly hand him his contract of confidentiality and employment, so I can show him the main points, which he studies fully, but I am relieved when he eventually signs on the dotted line.

I decide to conclude the meeting by telling Greg, "I'm over the moon you've decided to join us and to ensure your life can change immediately, we will deposit half a million pounds into your bank account this evening". After all this is literally loose change where I come from, I also push my luck one more time, "this will immediately release the financial pressures at home and you can also hand in your notice immediately and tell them you are not going to work there anymore". I'm convinced that Greg is now tied to the company, some would say committed, but I would say indebted. More importantly, we have Greg in the palm of our hands and ready to start work immediately.

Thirty One

What a day yesterday was and I'm already back in my office. I've reported to everyone that Greg is all signed up and is already heading back to Tx3 this morning. I also have the security team watching his every move on our systems and they confirm he is arriving shortly. The gates are opened just in time for him to swoop straight in and I then receive a call to confirm he is outside. I walk to meet him and give him a friendly hug and kiss as I am told, this is how people greet each other in 2019. Clearly things will be different in 2020 and even more different again in 2102. If I'm being honest it is also very nice to have skin to skin contact once again. "Welcome back so soon Greg, I knew you wouldn't be able to resist the lure of the job and the anticipation of your first project", I proudly announce. "Come and have a cup of tea and a catch up, I have someone I want you to meet, someone who will be giving you all the details for your first target and someone who I believe you will learn to rely on".

As we settle in, there is a knock on the door and Christian walks in. This slightly annoys me, I was only introduced as his new boss a few days ago and yet he just swans into my office like he owns the place. Christian is full of bravado and he and Greg chat about the job and how it will all work. I am distracted by a message on my phone telling me, to get Greg working immediately. It states, we will send him on a very low risk job first, so he can learn how it's done, he will be able to gain experience and more importantly confidence in himself. There's another job, we then need to squeeze in after this one, which is vital to generating income. However, I need you to meet with me later to discuss the big picture and the main job he's been employed to do. You will find me on sub level 1, regards, Ms Rees.

As I rejoin the conversation, Christian is asking if he even needs to answer Greg's last question? Which is difficult as I have not caught any of the discussion. Instead I avoid it by saying, "Greg knows what's happening here, don't you"? Followed by instructing them to head for the debrief rooms and start getting ready, "as we'd like to get Greg moving today with his first job". As they leave, I collect my things and head to meet Ms Rees, as instructed.

As the lift doors open I am met by a tough looking security lady, carrying a weapon. "Ms Rees is expecting you, follow me". As I wander behind her, I wonder if this person is from the here and now, or if she has also been brought in from a previous generation. I am soon ushered into an office, which has no windows to the outside world and is filled with artificial light. "I hope you have Greg working already"? Is my unfriendly welcome! I am about to answer, when I realise it is a rhetorical question and any answer I may give will be irrelevant. Ms Rees is already moving on to the business part of the meeting. "We have a far more important job to discuss", followed by her gesture for me to take a seat. "Our next job is to repat John Lennon, he can clearly write a song or two and we urgently need more income. We have promised the record labels a few brilliant songs to pass to them within the next month or two. They have a few new artists that require new material, so we need to expedite our plans. This move will keep the wolves from our door, so to speak. We do have a challenge to overcome, in that we don't actually have anyone to pull the trigger though. We can't afford for it to be Greg, as that will ruin everything we've worked hard to achieve. I am hoping you will have the solution, if not I need to approach the post generation council and I fear they are running out of patience to my requests". It is at this very moment that I know I have the perfect solution, but executing it will be a little more challenging. "Please leave this one with me, I believe I have the very person, I just need to set it up".

Ms Rees seems pleased and immediately moves to the next point. "Once we have our Mr Lennon situation resolved, we urgently need to move on to our main goal". We both know what this is and the importance of getting it right. "Do we know who the target is yet"? Is my slightly forward question. Ms Rees nods, "yes but it's a need to know basis and right now you don't need to know, now go and resolve our first issue, one step at a time".

It is very apparent that this meeting is over, so I leave immediately. A few hours later, I receive a call to confirm Greg has already completed his first job and is heading to his new office. I immediately go to meet him and knock on his glass door, "Congratulations on a very successful first assignment, did you enjoy it"? I ask, as Greg looks incredibly happy, but proud is the overwhelming look I see in him. "It was fantastic, it took a couple of weeks to get it sorted, but I'm very pleased it all worked out in the end, Christian tells me John will be with us tomorrow, which is amazing and I guess exciting for the next stage". I am genuinely pleased for Greg, he's clearly worked hard on this case and is getting the rewards, "this one successful mission means hundreds of thousands of people should now benefit from his arrival". This in part is true, but isn't anywhere near as important as the forthcoming jobs. I tell Greg about the job earmarked for John and swiftly move to getting Greg home to his family, as they haven't seen him for a few hours, I joke. In reality I need to head back home myself, in order to resolve our issue with finding a shooter for John Lennon.

Thirty Two

I place myself in the private area at the rear of the office, close the door and hit the boomerang. I am of course, immediately back, looking at my team and receive a smiling, welcoming look, from Denise. We have been a team for a few years now and have grown a very close friendship. We both know all about the challenges in each other's lives and have a proper female support system in place for each other. I know for certain that I can rely on her, more than anyone else in this World. This is why I'd told Greg that I am sure he will learn to rely on Christian. The bond has to be solid between each other for this team to be successful, so the correct pairing is an essential part of the recruitment process. Den and I both know that this is our most important job yet, which means a huge amount of pressure, or the human race literally expires. "How'd you get on"? Denise asks, "Wow Den", I start, "I've only just put my feet on the ground". I chuckle, "yeah all good, Greg is on board and has completed his first job already, he's a quick learner that one. He has a worldly way about him as well, he just adapts to any given situation, I'm genuinely impressed. Anyway, we have another situation to resolve before I head back. Ms Rees", I say shaking my head sarcastically, "wants us to find the John Lennon shooter"! Den just stares at me, "you're not thinking what I'm thinking are you? How are you going to pull that off"? I smile a knowing sort of smile, Mark will be the perfect person for the job and we both know the reasons why. As I walk towards the wash down room, Den follows me in.

As soon as we shut the door, to the only room in the building that isn't monitored, or bugged, she starts, "you need to be really careful here, you can't afford any slip ups, or you'll have a few people wanting your blood". I instinctively hug Den, "thank you but we both know this is the only way".

Following my shower and a fresh pair of clothes, I feel comfortable again. Those clothes from the olden days are pretty uncomfortable, they look stylish but they are not for me. I head back to my office and call Mark, to get this set up. "Hey, do you fancy meeting me for some food, I have a very interesting proposal to discuss with you, which has literally just come my way"? Mark sounds very interested indeed and we agree to meet in an hour, in a little pasta place. I arrive a little early, so park across the street from the restaurant and watch as Mark arrives and enters first. I immediately follow him, so he isn't kept waiting too long, as I know how much this irritates him. I need to keep him in a happy place today, I need to keep him in the zone and I need to get his agreement.

As I open the door, Mark is stood there checking us in. He turns to see me enter and gives me a welcome kiss. Before he can say anything a waiter approaches and ushers us to our seats, presenting a menu for us to peruse. In fairness, I don't need to look at the menu, as I am going to have the delicious crab dish they serve here. Mark orders for us and we are all set. "So what's this interesting proposal that has come your way"? Mark asks immediately. My face lights up, as I am trying to convey it to be this amazing opportunity. "My boss has approached me to find a suitably trained gunman, someone who can take out a famous person and not let it affect them. I know you are keen to have a go at time travelling, so I immediately thought of you. We both know you have the right training for this and the beauty is the gunman will have notoriety forever sealed in the history books, as this event will happen back in 1980". Mark is instantly engaged, well of course I'm your man, but what's the pay and I need to know more about the plan. I chuckle and lean in to speak a little quieter, "the pay is simple, they've agree to pay fifty times what you earn right now, for the rest of your life, for this one time job. Once the job is complete you will need to hang around at the scene to get arrested, so the World knows who you are and have the proof of the murder. Then a few days later, we will collect you from prison to bring you home and you are then free for the rest of your life". Mark sips his drink while he thinks about it, "so how the hell do I get to 1980? I appreciate this is something you do all the time, but how do we actually do it"? This is a simple one, "we get you into my base, get you onto the platform and then you will be in 2019 instantly, with me. From there a team is already working on the target and once they are ready, we move you on to 1980, so you can do your thing".

Our food arrives and we tuck in, "we do however have one issue", I say, to further play to his ego. "There's a man called Greg who's working this case, he believes he will be bringing the target back, however we plan on double crossing him right at the end. We bring you in and tell him you are the better man for the job, which will not be a pretty meeting, but we need you to do this and not him, as we want someone who can do it right, what do you say"? Mark looks the cockiest I think I've ever seen him, "I'm in, but who's the target"? I smile and whisper, "some old time singer called John Lennon, apparently he was pretty famous in his day". I deliberately play it down, knowing damn well that Mark knows who he was, it is like lighting up a firework, as his face literally brightens with excitement, "Annie, you are a genius, of course I know who he is, I'm a huge fan of his work, I'm one hundred percent in. Do I need to sign anything"? "No there isn't anything to be signed, we don't want a paper trail on any of this", I confirm while tapping my nose. Mark is in the best mood I've seen him in for ages, he will do the job because his ego can't say no, which is perfect. We toast our drinks to the new job, Mark suddenly says, "come on let's head home, I'm taking you straight to bed, for the night of your life"! I play all girly, "aww ok then, but can we think about booking a second honeymoon when this is all done"? Mark agrees and we head off home shortly afterwards.

Thirty Three

The following morning I'm headed back into work, with the issue of who will pull the trigger and kill John Lennon resolved. I swan into work and Den is already waiting for me. "Well... how'd it go with Mark last night"? I smile a confident smile, "hook, line and sinker". Den however, looks concerned, "are you okay hun"? In fairness I'm happier than I've been in years and my face reflects this. Den confirms my next trip is a very quick one, "you need to see the arrival of Greg's target. Please can you praise Greg for a job well done, then get straight back here". Being the good employee that I am, I follow instructions dutifully. In and out quickly, "we can now concentrate of our Mr Lennon", Den announces, which I am more than ready for.

As I stand looking at Den, I wink, showing I am ready, probably more ready than I've been in years. Den acknowledges my confirmation and I am gone, or I should say I arrive, in the rear of my office ready to tackle the John Lennon case. As I open the door to the office, Ms Rees is sat waiting for me on the sofa with another person. "About time" she states, like they have been waiting hours, which is clearly not the case. "This is Dr Douglas, I personally employed her a few months ago and she will accompany us today, to keep an eye on things and to keep everyone on track". I smile my friendliest smile, "hello Dr Douglas and I'm pleased to meet you". I quickly move towards Ms Rees and confirm, "I have the solution to our shooter challenge. His name is Mark Chapman, a highly skilled gunman and I have his agreement to proceed, when we are ready". Ms Rees looks pleased with my progress. "Good, can you finalise the details with this Mark and have him here ready to start as soon as Greg gets everything in place"? I am pleased to confirm, "yes I will be able to move to the next stage after our meeting today, shall we head off to it now"? As we leave the office to find Greg, we talk about the job in hand and how this is a must succeed mission, how I need to apply the right amount of pressure on Greg to keep him motivated, as the three of us enter the meeting room.

Dr Douglas catches me by surprise as she immediately takes control of the room, clearly trying to impress her boss, "Good morning Greg we are here to put you through your paces and get you ready for your trip. I'm Doctor Douglas and I'm very pleased to be meeting you at long last,

I've heard about your last success already, congratulations".

Doctor Douglas then introduces Greg to Ms Rees, but being the ever self important person she is, she could only manage a nod in Greg's direction, but she doesn't actually say anything. Doctor Douglas eventually turns to look at Christian, "so you've obviously met this idiot then, no introduction is needed" and then towards me "and of course you already know the big bad boss". I am starting to feel pretty awkward at this point, so step in, "right, let's crack on then shall we everyone, let's pull up a chair and start throwing some ideas around. We need to know everything you have on our Mr Lennon, what the challenges are, as I'm sure there will be many and ideally some quick wins please. I have a meeting in an hour and a half and it will be good to at least road map the basic ideas of this project. We can all then head home, to get a good night sleep before working on the finer details tomorrow".

We get the basic plan mapped out, fairly quickly and as everyone leaves the meeting, I know exactly where I am heading. Straight back home, so I can finalise the John Lennon plans with my husband Mark. With slight trepidation I trigger the boomerang and I am back with Den, ready to get this thing resolved. We have the usual debrief with Den and the team and she cleverly only asks direct questions about the job, or Greg. Once done I am able to head home to an evening with Mark and to plan the next few days.

Mark, as ever is waiting for me in the window, behind twitching curtains, so I wave as I approach. As I breeze in through the front door, he is ready with his usual questions, "where have you been today? How long were you there? Who did you meet", it is always very tedious, but getting this out of the way, I am able to turn the discussion to his new job. "There have been some developments today, Greg has started his work, so we are very close to bringing you in now. Greg doesn't know anything and the next time I visit I will explain how you fit into this picture, I'm not sure Greg will fully understand, but that's his problem right"? Mark is full of himself, "I'm basically the main man on this job aren't I, without me, this whole thing falls apart doesn't it"? I was ready for this self importance and ready to just suck it up, especially if it means getting the result I need. The night goes much smoother than I have been used to recently, with Mark lauding himself around and I confirm he needs to get ready, as he will be drafted in soon.

My alarm soon wakes me in the morning and despite feeling exhausted I am ready. I need to return to Tx3 to keep everything on track. Den arrived to set up, before me as always, it definitely feels like she does all the work and I just claim the rewards. "Hey, what a lovely day this is", I happily chirp on my arrival, "possibly the best day ever", comes Den's response. I know this is a big trip this time and I am determined to hit the ground running. We have prepared for this and I can't do anymore now, I just need to be the best me possible. I quickly find my usual spot and Den nods, a good luck sort of nod and that's it, I am back in 2019. I immediately call Christian to join me, I want to be as fully informed as possible today and I don't need any surprises. Christian briefs me on the previous trip Greg took to Scotland and the plan for today. I am satisfied they are doing all they can at this stage and tell Christian I will be joining them this morning.

Once the time arrives, I leave my office and head down a long corridor where I catch up with Christian and Greg, "I do like to be here, it's much more exciting than spreadsheets", I state upon reaching them, "besides a few hours or even days away for you, is only a few seconds of my time, which is perfect. Christian has already brought me up to speed, first thing this morning, it's a critical visit this time right? as they all are I suppose".

Christian clearly feels the need to announce the plan again, even though we had gone over it earlier, maybe this is for Greg's benefit. Either way, this is my opportunity to slip in some information while Greg is focusing on the job at hand, "go and get your target and when you get back I need to introduce you to someone called Mark, who may or may not be able to help with this case. Mark is going to be seconded to us from the CIA in a joint project. He is flying in from Beirut where he's been training and the CIA feel he might be able to help us out with this particular job. Anyway if he's around I will introduce you to him, but I just wanted you to be aware in case you bump into him". Greg appears too focused on the job to really care, which is perfect and he is soon off getting ready. If I could pat myself on the back then I would.

I arrive just in time to see Greg leaving on his next trip and immediately join Christian ahead of his return. Christian quickly announces that Greg is already incoming and then he's here in front of us once again. I love this technology it is just perfect.

Greg and Christian chat, before Greg asks "can you send me straight back to the 9th of February 1961"? I step forward about to speak, when Ms Rees suddenly speaks up from behind us asking, "but the bigger question is not what date, but where would you need to go? I mean where are we sending you? After all the World is an awfully big place, you could be sent to my favourite place, Las Vegas, or Brighton as an example". I realise this isn't about asking a reasonable question, this is about letting me know who's boss around here and keeping me firmly in my place. After a little back and forth, Christian stands back from his laptop smiling and announces, "of course it is, I should have known, it's soo friggin obvious". I on the other hand don't like this sort of macho bravado time wasting crap that he is displaying, so immediately ask, "Well, come on then, are you going to share"? Christian eventually confirms the location as Liverpool, in The Cavern Club, like it is the holy grail or something.

As Greg positions himself, my mind drifts back to Mark, getting him inside this operation and getting this job finished, before realising Greg has already gone, again. Christian is already announcing his return, it is almost like blink and you'll miss it. But what appears in front of us, shakes me to the core. Greg appears with blood dripping from him and without thinking I launch into, "What have you done"? Greg is clearly trying to be macho with his sarcastic reply, about having a fight with a fork. I rush towards Greg, frantic that he has ballsed the whole thing up, asking, "but has the job been ruined"? Greg looks in pain, but confirms the operation is still in tact, which upon hearing this, my brain disengages for a moment, as I am relieved to hear the operation hasn't been ruined, but as my brain engages again, I suddenly remember I am supposed to be the one in charge here. I realise I need to show some empathy, "sorry Greg, of course I am very concerned about you as well and we will need to get you all fixed up urgently". Greg snaps back, "I don't want to be fixed up, I really need to get back to John urgently, as the whole fork in hand, blood dripping things is the plan". I don't really understand what is happening, my brain can see the blood dripping from Greg, who is clearly in pain but I am confused. Greg can sense we are struggling, so he spells out the plan to us. Christian is already working on the next steps, just like Den would have done, these two are so alike, it must be a requirement for the job. October 1962 is discussed and a place called Nuneaton and in what feels like a whirlwind minute, is soon over as Greg is on his way once again. I am exhausted, just from watching it all unfold and actually appreciate the stress that the likes of Christian and Den must go through. I've only seen things from my side of the job before, how tiring the job can be, the days, or weeks that I am away and I've never really stopped to appreciate the other side of things.

The next thing I know, Greg is back again looking much happier and his hands are bandaged up. Greg tells us about the latest events and confirms he will be heading home. He has however, already agreed to meet up with John Lennon again on the 9th of February 1964. Christian doesn't need to be told twice and is already working on the next stages, while Greg insists on taking some time off. I too think this is a good idea as it will allow me time to head home and collect Mark to bring him here, ready for when the time is right. Having encouraged Greg to head home and relax I too will be headed home, but not to relax.

Thirty Four

I head back to my office and hit the boomerang once more. I am pleased to be back with Den and confirm the plan from this point. "You will return after this won't you"? Den asks, "I mean when this is all finished". I give Den a great big hug, mainly for my benefit if I'm being honest, but also to show her I really do care about her. "I'm not planning on leaving you here, by yourself, so let's hope this thing goes to plan". I shower, change quickly and head to security to authorise and collect the necessary clearance that Mark will need, for this to work. I call him, to confirm he needs to get himself here as soon as he can, we will be returning a week after I left, as this is the day we had all agreed on. I meet Mark at the main entrance about an hour later and update him. He changes into the clothes required for this job and confirms he has everything he needs, from an old gun to a book he is taking with him. "Why on earth are you taking a book", I enquire. Mark looks incredibly arrogant in his response, "because I want to create history and a legacy that will be talked about for years to come". I decide to just let him carry on and as we enter the main room, Den stands behind her systems, waiting for us. I position Mark ready and tell him "when you arrive I will already be there waiting for you. Den will make sure to program my arrival for a few seconds before you actually arrive". Mark nods in agreement but I can tell that all this technology is starting to hurt his brain, which I like, as I am now the one in control. Den pushes the button and he is gone. As I stand ready for my turn, Den says, "you do know he hasn't had the boomerang installed don't you, this really is a one way trip for him". I step back off the platform, "Den, he may be my husband but I hate every fibre of his being, he has abused me for years, at one point I thought I would be broken forever, but this is my one chance to get my life back on track and I'm going to take it". A tear rolls down my cheek, "one way or another I'm getting out of this marriage today, so let's get me out of here". Den smiles a caring best friend smile and sets the system, I wipe away my tears, as I don't want anything to ruin this now. Den confirms we are good to go and presses the button, while holding up her hand as if gesturing goodbye. I arrive in the private room at the rear of the office and I am able to turn around, just in time to see Mark arriving. "I told you I'd be right here waiting for you", I confirm, to ensure Mark doesn't suspect any funny business. We move straight into the main part of the office and go over the plans fully, before we head down to the main room. "When we get in there, we need to mingle, as we have invited lots of people to witness this auspicious day and we must remain professional at all times. I will introduce you to Greg when he arrives and I will need to put on a bit of a show for the investors. Your job is to remain calm and collected, so no one suspects anything, agreed"? Mark nods in agreement, but with an evil glint in his eye, which certainly doesn't make me feel any more in control.

We arrive in the main room which, as planned, is already full. I instantly switch to professional Annie, mixing and chatting with people. Mark doesn't leave my side, watching every move I make and listening to every word I say. He is suffocating me, literally sucking the life out of me, but I can feel the air of hope inching towards me as every second passes. I suddenly notice Greg entering the room, so I quickly remind Mark to remain professional and I step onto my stage to perform. "Good morning Greg", I deliberately say loudly in order to capture the rooms attention. With open arms, I confirm, "everyone, this is Greg", and I start to clap, as a prompt for everyone to follow, which they do. I move towards Greg and immediately guide him towards an important investor, as I'm keen to impress. I am however, very much aware of how close Mark is to me, almost shadow like, as I sense him right on my shoulder. I can almost feel his breath on my neck, so decide it will be better to introduce Mark to Greg quickly. Turning I state, "This is Mark, he's on secondment from the CIA, I think I mentioned him to you the other day". Greg appears to have no idea what is happening in this room, but to my relief he shakes hands with Mark anyway. I feel sick in my stomach and Greg confirms, "Annie has indeed mentioned you to me. Annie says you'll be with us for a short time". Mark stares at Greg constantly, as if trying to antagonise him, "yes a short time, but I'm not sure how long yet, could be my last day today, it just depends on where my services are required and when really". I am about to ask Greg how he feels about today, but he quickly says, "well it was nice to meet you Mark, but I need to check in with Christian". I smile, pleased that Greg is moving away from Mark so soon and before Mark can cause any problems. I don't have long though, before a second investor and personal friend of Ms Rees appears, clearly very happy to be meeting the soon to be infamous Mark Chapman.

Despite making lots of small talk with various people, I am very much aware that Greg and Christian have been gone for a while. This makes me anxious, I try to remain calm, but the nerves and emotions are definitely getting to me. After what feels like hours, Greg and Christian reenter the room. All the guests follows Greg's every move as they instinctively move to the fringes of the room, well away from the main platform. Greg positions himself and despite the noise levels in the room he avidly studies Christian, awaiting his direction and then he's gone from our sight. The room gasps, as if viewing the most magical of shows and then an eerie silence falls over the room like a cloak enveloping the space. Christian confirms almost immediately, that Greg is returning and as he reappears, the room erupts once again. My eyes immediately lock directly onto Greg's, like a heat seeking missile, which gives me goosebumps on my arms and along the spine of my back. Despite all the people in the room we instinctively find each other and Greg nods at me, confirming John has agreed to the repat. It's done, we are ready to get John back to Tx3, but more importantly I am about to get rid of this complete pig of a man from my life forever. I immediately confirm to the repat team, that they are clear to dispatch. Despite feeling completely overwhelmed I give a slight cough, to clear my throat and announce like some kind of circus ring master, "Ladies and gentlemen, what Greg has been able to achieve is incredibly valuable for us all here at Tx3, but invaluable for the future generations. Please take a short break and when you return, we will ask you to stand at the other side of this glass wall, as we want to welcome our guest into a calm environment. But ladies and gentlemen, today we will be welcoming the one and only, Mr John Lennon". I find myself barely able to breath as everyone claps and starts to leave the room, including Mark, who for the first time ever is following my instructions. Leaving only a handful of us here, the inner sanctum if you will, to tell Greg about the next stage.

Christian, myself and of course Ms Rees who insists on being involved in everything, all gather around Greg. We all stand silently at first, listening to Greg as he debriefs us. I confirm the repat team have been instructed, as I struggle to hold in the waves of emotions I'm feeling. I continue, "Greg we need you here to welcome Mr Lennon, as you did for your last John". Greg is clearly very unhappy, confused and angrily states, "of course I am going to be here". I continue, "we will be sending another member of the team to physically remove John". But before I can finish, a bullish Greg interjects, "remove him, I assume you mean collect him"? This makes me incredibly uncomfortable and I look towards Ms Rees for support, "No, I did mean remove him, we need him here, so we can get him rehabilitated as quickly as possible, so we can move forwards". Again I glance at Ms Rees, as Greg continues to challenge, "who is going to remove him"? I know it is down to me to confirm as firmly as I can, "we will be sending our CIA colleague, Mark, as he has been trained for these exact situations". I am relieved to feel my phone buzz, with confirmation that the repat has been successful and we are now good to go.

Everyone starts to file back into the main room and they dutifully line up behind the glass wall, out of the way, as instructed. Mark follows them in, but turns to enter the main chamber and the hatred I feel towards this man almost bubbles over. I can't stand the way he walks, the way he smirks in his arrogant style. He even has the audacity to wink at me, subtle but domineering, as he tucks the stupid book into his pocket. Little does he know, he will be doing a lot more reading where he is going. Mark walks towards us and baits Greg with, "don't worry Greg I will take good care of John", while patting his arm as a show of masculinity. Greg struggles to understand what is happening, but does manage to say, "have a good trip, we can catch up when you get back". Mark looks at him like he is a piece of shit on his shoe and chuckles, "yeah when I'm back". I am very worried that this could turn ugly and ruin all my hard fought plans, so I quickly jump in with, "come on you two, stop the gossiping, we have a job to do". I immediately take Mark over to the launch platform, ready for him to head off.

Christian confirms he is ready and Mark nods in agreement. The thirty second warning rings out around the room and I feel like my heart might just stop and I need to remind myself to breath. I am very close to ending all my pain and suffering and the beginning of a new life is almost within touching distance, if it works. I am certainly struggling to hold it all together, when Christian announces, five seconds, four, three, two, one and Mark is gone. Not just gone from this time period, not just gone from sight but gone from my life forever. I let out a strange noise and a heavy breath fills my lungs, as if filling me me with hope and promise to what the future holds. I've done it, I have finally done it, Mark shitface Chapman will rot in prison for the rest of his life and there is nothing he can do about it. I am experiencing an out of body experience, one of euphoria and relief mixed with complete peace and calmness. Christian interrupts this special moment, by announcing John Lennon is arriving and I have to switch back to business mode once more. With that John Lennon appears right before my eyes, shocked and scared as he holds his arms against his body, as if shielding himself from pain. I am still an emotional wreck when John shouts, "Yeah", making me jump and shake, then bizarrely he shouts "Yeah", for a second time. John turns to survey the room quickly, looking for what turns out to be Greg as they grab hold of each other, tears streaming down their faces. They fall to the floor crying and speaking to each other in one conjoined emotional heap. I am a shaking mess from the whirlwind of emotions, as I receive a tap on my arm by one of the medical team, waiting for my instruction to intervene. I give the confirmation and they move in to collect and remove John to the S.H.

Christian rushes to Greg and this again confirms the bond they have formed with each other. My heart is pounding, tears are running down my face, but not out of empathy for Greg and John, but sheer selfish relief of my own successful closure. I quickly wipe away my tears as I walk towards Greg, "that was one hell of an emotional reaction, you both have clearly bonded. Thank goodness you were here to greet him, or we would have a major incident on our hands". I can see Ms Rees also approaching, out of the corner of my eye, to say, "well done Greg, you've proved today that you were one hundred percent the right person for the job. I'm literally still shaking", holding out her hands as if to offer proof. I for one, am not buying this act, but maybe it shows she can be nice at times.

I start to think about heading back home, so I can tell Den everything, when Greg suddenly asks, "but where is Mark"? I try to play this down, acting oblivious at first, in the hopes the question will go away, "Mark? what do you mean"? Greg however isn't going to let this one go, "Mark, you know, the guy you sent to remove John". I really want to tell them all about my shitty life with Mark and how I only did it this way so I could set him up, but no one can ever know. As this flashes through my brain, Ms Rees answers for me, "Mark won't be returning to us for a while, he is being detained you see. At some point in the near future Annie will get him released and send him off to do another job, but right now, he's not coming back". Greg continues questioning, "why"? again Ms Rees continues, "that's because he is the person that killed John Lennon and he was arrested at the scene". It's like I'm a witness in court, hearing the sentence being handed down to Mark and I am struggling to hold in my relief and joy. Greg still pursuing this, "Hang on a minute, are you telling me that we were the ones who killed John Lennon, if you hadn't sent Mark, whatever his name is, today, then John would still be alive and could have lived to an old age? why? why did we kill John Lennon at such a young age"? I sense the true Ms Rees returning from her minor relapse, as she is clearly getting bored of Greg now, "because we need him here right now, to help us make many millions in revenue, which keep you and everyone in work. It also means we can then have enough funding to go on with this project and save many many more people from history! It was a necessary evil I'm afraid and you did a perfect job today in saving our future generations".

Thirty Five

I'm exhausted and emotionally drained from the events of this past week. Deep down I know I should head back home, to see Den and start putting my life back in order, but instead I head back to the place I've been staying in recently. I practically fall through the front door as I burst into tears, tears of relief, tears of joy and tears of pure exhaustion. I am also able to laugh a little from the feeling of excitement, as I've finally got my life back on track. Technically by now, Mark is already dead, as he is stuck in 1980 and I live just over one hundred and twenty years in the future. This thought fills me with a warm fuzzy feeling, one I've never enjoyed before, like a comfort blanket wrapping itself around me to sooth away my pain. I pour myself a well earned glass of wine and pull up a chair right in front of the window, overlooking the river and the expensive restaurants. I'm just going to sit here sipping and staring out at this beautiful World and for the first time in years, I make time for myself. Time to breath and relax, time to switch off from the World and time to just be in my own thoughts and plans for the future and for the first time in years I am content.

The morning soon appears, I'm a little groggy from the wine, but ready to start my new life. Not that anyone will even realise that this is a momentous day for me. As I get myself settled in to my office, I'm pretty certain that when Greg arrives, he will want to see John Lennon and I need to make sure he doesn't suspect anything. I set about checking his status, which is confirmed as a pass, with John receiving a clean bill of health. John is apparently keen to start work immediately, he's very upbeat and the team confirm, this is a good sign of a successful repat. I therefore authorise Greg for a visit upon his arrival today. After all, it's better for Greg to see John in a controlled hospital setting. After today, John will be placed in his section pod and set to work with the others.

Everything is now all set for Greg's arrival and I am ready to discuss yesterday's events with him, knowing I need to get him back on side. He will no doubt be confused from the whole saga that unfolded. I need to approach today, by being completely honest with Greg, or in reality, playing at honesty, as there is a lot that Greg can never know. I receive the message that Greg is arriving, so pull myself together and head to meet him. As both he and Christian enter the building I am determined to be upbeat, "Good morning you lazy pair, how are you feeling today"? Greg replies,

"I'm very tired, mentally exhausted and confused, but I wanted to see if could meet up with John today, to see how he is settling in, if that's okay"? I happily confirm, "I knew that's what you would want, so I've already sent the request through and the reply was positive, but you've been asked to keep the visit short, as John recovers from this stressful transition". This is an easy win for me as Greg replies, "absolutely, I don't want to stress him out, I just want to make sure he's fine, when can I go to him"? This is certainly a good positive step to repairing the damage from yesterday, "right now if you want to"? I reply, followed quickly by asking, "Christian will you show Greg the way down to sub-level 4 please". The two of them leave immediately, like two naughty school boys rushing to get away from the head mistress and then I am alone again.

It's not long however, before there is a knock at my door and Christian leans around it, letting himself in. "Do you make a habit of just letting yourself in"? I ask, in a passive aggressive tone, which Christian clearly doesn't understand, or he just decides to ignore. I can see that he is clearly not going away, so I ask, "What can I do for you"? Christian's appearance isn't very friendly, as he approaches my desk. I gesture for him to take a seat, but he remains standing. "I've come to explain a few things to you", is his opener, which in fairness does catch my attention. "Greg has worked his friggin butt off for you and this company since he arrived. He has not questioned any of the instructions and has learned the job in an unbelievably quick time frame. Much quicker than any of his predecessors and he has achieved the results you need. Yesterday was horrible, at no point did Greg or myself know what was happening and we were essentially a circus show. This is not only a joke it is a very dangerous way to work and I for one think you owe us both an apology. As I am here, I would also like some reassurance that this will not be how we do things in the future, if you can't agree to this, then I'm out of here". I realise just how close they have become, they have each others backs and I can definitely see myself and Den in this pairing. I also have to get Christian back on track, if I stand any chance of keeping Greg. "There are clearly a lot of things happening in the background which, you and others will not be privy to. You will naturally have been shielded from this sort of detail and this is how it has always been. However Christian, just because it has always been that way, doesn't mean it needs to carry on in this way either and for that I am sorry. I will make sure things change around here and when I get the chance I will also apologise to Greg". Despite Christians rough edges, I am actually impressed with his directness and his protectiveness of Greg. If however, this meeting had been held with Ms Rees, he would have almost certainly lost his job. He had no way of knowing how I would react, being his new boss, but out of loyalty to Greg he came in here anyway, which I admire. It feels good to clear the air and Christian leaves the office much happier than when he arrived.

A little while later, I receive a message to confirm the John Lennon visit was a success and Greg is currently walking around the gardens. I call Ms Rees to confirm the job is now complete and to advise we are ready to move on to the next job. Ms Rees replies, "I must confess to being fairly satisfied with your results and yes we are ready for you to move to the next job, I will send over the file now, remember this is highly confidential". I feel proud to have reached this point, but I'm also aware that this is really only the beginning.

I message Greg, requesting he meets me in my office. I dangle the prospect of his next John, to get his brain active again. It's only a few minutes before Greg knocks on my door and leans around it at the same time, almost like Christian did earlier. Strangely though, I don't mind Greg doing it. How can two people do the exact same thing, but only one of them annoy me? "Oh come on in Greg", I announce, in my friendliest voice, "How are you feeling now"? Greg doesn't appear a hundred percent and confirms, "I'm okay, it's been a hard few days I guess , with plenty to think about, but I'm okay". I like Greg, he certainly wears his heart on his sleeve, but isn't rude, or arrogant with it, in fact he is the complete opposite of Mark. He is dependable, likeable, attractive and very loyal to those who he's made a commitment, which I appreciate and want to acknowledge.

This is my chance to be open with him, so we head toward the sofa, for a more relaxed setting. "We want you to be happy here and you've certainly settled in extremely well. We know how tough this job can be and I'm sorry I couldn't share the full information with you about Mark and the outcome.

I realise now that this was a mistake and I'm sorry for that. Christian has brought me right up to speed about the work you've done, how we can fully trust you and in the future I will make sure you are included in all aspects of your case. We all make mistakes from time to time, but I suppose the key thing is to admit when we are wrong and to learn from our mistakes. I am keen for this team to be together for many years, with you leading it, based on your experiences, especially those from recent times. I guess you would have learned a lot and how to apply those things in the future? Look, we aren't saying we are perfect, but I am keen to avoid a blame culture, so if anything is wrong, we need to talk about it, my door is always open for you. We can discuss, analyse and make corrections, so we can hopefully, avoid doing the same things again. Agreed"? I even put my hand out to shake on it. I've seen films from the old days where they even spat on their hands first, but think this is a step too far. Greg states firmly, "agreed" and I can feel the bad air lifting between us, "good, now let's clean the slate and move on to the next job shall we. Are you ready to start right back at the beginning"?

Greg is keen to move on, but stresses he needs a few days off, which I am happy to authorise. I know what it's like to be in this job and you must be one hundred percent committed, to perform. It is at this moment I remember the company holiday island and home, which everyone at a certain level has used, including myself from time to time. Everyone that's used it, has been told by their boss that it is their private island and have loved their time there. "Why don't you fly your family to my private island for the week"? I suddenly spout out, like I am the big boss around here, which to Greg, I suppose I am. "You can have access to my private jet and pilot, as I'm not going anywhere this week. There's everything there that you are going to need, for a great family break". Greg is clearly keen to use it and following some polite discussion, it's agreed. I just need to get this authorised now and quickly. If push comes to shove, I will just return to 2102 and deny all knowledge of the conversation. I practically push Greg out of the door and hastily call for assistance. I am relived to hear it will be authorised immediately, after all, I am the boss and what the boss wants, the boss gets.

Feeling pretty good about myself, I decide to stay here a little longer. My life is certainly better for me in this day and age, despite the obvious pressures from Ms Rees. I need to be here anyway, to tackle the biggest job of our lives, the job that has to succeed, or civilisation could be wiped out. I also know that for this to work, I will be accompanying Greg from here on in, after all, two heads are better than one. I like Greg and I'm confident we will make a great team a great time travelling duo. With that Greg calls me, "I just wanted to say thanks again, for the use of your island, I've just spoken with Bonnie and she is over the moon". I can't help but chuckle down the phone, "I'm just really pleased its all worked out for you, you deserve a break and we will definitely get more out of you when your back so don't worry, it's a win, win. By the way I didn't tell you about your next John, did I". Greg is horrified, "Oh my God you're right, I'm so sorry, I was too wrapped up in my own life". Greg is such an open book and it's a refreshing change from everyone else, "honestly it's not a problem and in fairness we will need the next few days, to get this one all mapped out, it's not going to be easy at all". Greg is clearly biting at the bit, "so who's my next John". I deliberately stall with the response, before confirming, "Greg, your next John, or should I say our, next John is the scientist Rosalind Franklin".

The End